Catherine S Lawrence

Autobiography. Sketch of Life and Labors of Miss Catherine S.

Lawrence

Catherine S Lawrence

Autobiography. Sketch of Life and Labors of Miss Catherine S. Lawrence

ISBN/EAN: 9783337125509

Printed in Europe, USA, Canada, Australia, Japan

Cover: Foto ©Raphael Reischuk / pixelio.de

More available books at **www.hansebooks.com**

AUTOBIOGRAPHY.

SKETCH OF

LIFE AND LABORS

OF

Miss Catherine S. Lawrence,

WHO

In Early Life Distinguished Herself as a Bitter Opponent
of Slavery and Intemperance, and Later in Life as
a Nurse in the Late War; and for Other
Patriotic and Philanthropic Services.

REVISED EDITION.

ALBANY, N. Y.
JAMES B. LYON, PRINTER,
1896.

INTRODUCTION.

The writer of the following pages having been
solicited frequently by her friends and by members of
the Grand Army corps to give her life and her labors
in the army to the public, has, after long consideration, consented, though somewhat reluctantly, to
do so.

The writer of this preface has acquainted himself
quite thoroughly with this little volume while in its
manuscript form, and he is prepared to pronounce it
a highly interesting work and well adapted to pro-
mote christianity and good morals, such as can be
introduced safely into the best and most refined
families or libraries in the land.

The authoress claims to be a lineal descendant of
Capt. Lawrence of the frigate *Chesapeake*, and she
frequently applies to herself throughout this work
the words used by that hero of the war of 1812,
" Don't give up the ship." The indomitable pluck
which seems to have characterized her career from
childhood to a period of over three score and ten,
is evidence of her having descended from a noble
ancestry. Thus in her case tradition is confirmed
by inheritance.

The publication cannot fail to be read with especial
interest by all who were actively engaged in putting

down the late Rebellion. This book should have a large sale and wide circulation, not only on account of its fearless advocacy of truth and of its rigorous denunciation of injustice of every form, but because of the material aid which the sale will secure to her, as she approaches the end of the voyage of life.

The government has not been as liberal with her, by way of awarding a pension, as it has in many other instances much less deserving. Her pension of twelve dollars per month is not large enough to furnish her with the common comforts of life, as every impartial judge must admit. It is hoped and expected that the proceeds of the sale of this work will so supplement this pittance, which she receives from the government, as that life's sunset shall be undimmed by the mists of anxiety and unobscured by the clouds of want.

CHESTER HARRIS.

ALBANY, *April* 20, 1893.

CHAPTER I.

"Each morning sees some task begin,
    Each evening sees it close ;
  Something attempted, something done,
    Has earned a night's repose." — *Longfellow*.

After disposing of my first edition many of my friends and readers urged me to give them more of my real life. My reply was that time and means had both been limited, but I would give them more in my next edition. Consequently I add to my book, sketch by sketch, and will commence by relating an incident connected with a recent visit.

I had been invited to spend the day with a family of old friends. Mother, son and myself were pleasantly seated conversing on different topics, when in came another member of the family — a professional gentleman. After shaking hands cordially he accosted me with, "I am mad at you, Kate ; I am going to quarrel with you."

I felt a queer sensation at the top of my head. It must be that the roots of my hair are disturbed. Quickly recovering myself I said :

" Madness, doctor, means hydrophobia, and if we are to quarrel, doctor, sit down and let's have a pleasant time of it."

" Well, I have read your book three times through."

"And that is what gave you the hydrophobia, is it?"

"No," said he, "I approve of it, but there is not enough of it. Why did you not give us more of your real life?"

"Yes," said I, "but the book, even before reading, has brought an epidemic of hydrophobia to some portions of our city, especially among the managers of our charitable institutions; but perhaps another dose of the same medicine might prove an antidote for the ill effects of the first. But if I were to give you the details of my whole life it would fill a volume as large as Webster's Lexicon. Then nobody would read it. Now the book is of a readable size. Then, you know, it is altogether disagreeable to look in a mirror and behold nothing but our own deformities. Satan is said to keep his cloven foot well covered, lest it proclaim him Satan, when he would pass as a saint, and, if my book should prove like a mirror, the more there is of it the more aggravating it might be, unless it might also give us some suggestions of reform."

CHAPTER II.

"For the soul is dead that slumbers
And things are not what they seem." — *Longfellow.*

In the morning of life we are very unsuspecting creatures. All things are just what they appear to be.

The artless child dreams of no disagreement between the apparent and the real; but before the sun has reached its zenith, and while it is yet fore- noon, we are cruelly surprised to find that " it is not all gold that glitters," and our diamonds prove too frequently to be but burnished brass.

Who of us, even as children, have not found our- selves sadly mistaken in our estimate of people and things? When character and quality have proved a failure, our supposed jewels only worthless peb- bles, our beautiful things but deformities, and dis- appointments have seemed almost to crush our young hearts, and drive us back within ourselves, until we fairly recoil from the touch of humanity, we become so distrustful and cynical that we feel prone to let faith drop entirely and drift with the tide. Like the little girl, who, upon finally learning that Santa Claus was only a myth, lost faith in her parents, and coming to her mother, said: "So there is no Santa Claus after all, and it is only you and papa who fill my stockings on Christmas?" "I suppose so," her mother replied; when the child with childish disgust said, "And I don't suppose there is any God either; you have probably been fooling me about that too."

This loss of faith in childhood, this finding out that older people are not so good and pure as we have thought them to be, is one primal means of sending many a little boy and girl to the bad, and ultimately filling our prisons and electric chairs.

It is so extremely difficult to distinguish between

the false and the genuine that we are constantly mourning over disappointments from misplaced confidence and treacherous friendships. What we want and what we need is more real life and more of real truth in our lives.

CHAPTER III.

" Two tender feet upon the untried border
Of life's mysterious land." — *Anon.*

The little girl of Mr. L. has strayed away. The villagers and lower neighborhood are all out searching the woods and farm, and draining the raceways and flumes, but have found no trace of the child. The raceway leading from the upper mill to the oil mill below is about an eighth of a mile. This was thoroughly searched, every corner of the mills was gone over, the company was about giving up the search and were fearful that she must have gone to the large stream, which was very high at this time. It would be very difficult to find her. Just at this time Mrs. S., who was living on the bank near by, as she was walking along, noticed some little doll's garments fastened on the hooks of the tender bars. She thought for a moment, " this is Kittie's work. She has surely gone to the large stream and is drowned! Before I see her mother I'll go down the bank and see if I can find any traces of her." Very soon she found little footprints in the sand. " Now I'll see where she found her way into the water ; working my way through the brushes, I came to a large flat stone projecting into the water, and there lay the little adventuress fast asleep with a doll garment in one hand, the other under her head." Mrs. S. looked at her a moment and said to herself, " Well, you are a little body, but you have raised a regiment who are fighting for you on land and water!" She caught her up and carried her up on the bank, held her with one hand and raised her up in sight, and the nearest gun was fired which gave the signal that the child was found. All this time Kittie was improving her lungs in high soprano, and was taken to her mother.

Among the workmen was a fine musician who taught dancing school in winter and worked in the shop the rest of the year. He had a long table in the shop and on this he gave Kittie lessons in dancing. She had an outfit of tight pants made of red pressed cloth, a sailor jacket and soldier cap. She was fond of dancing and made great progress. She had no playmates, being the youngest of twelve children, and those living were grown to man and womanhood, and some were married. But Kittie would always find something to amuse herself with. One day, after her mother had dressed her nicely, she went out to catch birds, as she called them; found a large number gathered around a mud puddle. She approached them softly with her apron uplifted, fell upon them, as she thought, but her butterflies were not to be caught, but Kittie was in a sad plight; her face and dress were covered with mud!

Kittie had a place of punishment, a little stair-way room with a stool in it; in this she was put, sometimes for a half hour or more or less, according as her disobedience demanded. This was called by Kittie her jail-house. When she saw herself covered with mud she knew that she was now to go to her place of punishment. Off she started and entered her jail-house unperceived. She remained there until the regiment was on duty. She opened the door softly, peeped out her head; her mother looked up, saw the little fright and almost fainted, saying: " Kitty, is that you ?" " Tesmam." " Where have you been ?" " In my dail-house." " Who put you there?" " My own self." " What made you go there?" " Tause I was naughty and dot muddy." " And then you went into your jail-house?" " Tesmam." " Well, something must be done with you, my lady, this will never do; every few days the whole place is in an uproar in looking after you — the workmen have to quit their work and lose three or four hours to find you." " Will oo teep me in my dail-house, mama, and may Wooly tay by me ?" All this time Kittie was going through a process of having the mud washed from her head and face which had dried on. Her father comes in. " What in this world is the matter now with my little girl?" " Yes," said her mother, " look at her, she was mud all over catching butter-flies." " Yes, papa, I dust went in my dail-house a drate while." " Yes, my little heroine, and had a regiment at your command ; you shall have a ride with me to-morrow. She has to do something, she has no one to play with her but Wooly, her cat." "Yes, papa, Wooly is so dood, tan her go riding to-morrow?" "No, Kittie, she can't ride horse-back; I can't hold her and you both on the horse." The next day Kittie had a fine ride on horseback with her father. She said: "Papa, they tant put me in my dail-house to-day; nor they tant hunt for me tause I taint there."

Kittie and her cat were constant companions; Wooly could open the doors and walk in at any time. Her father was expected to be out the coming night until a late hour and gave orders to leave the back hall door unlocked. That night after the family had retired the mother awoke and heard the rattling of the room door-latch. She listened but heard no footsteps. She became alarmed, arose and stepped out into the hall and called up the help; the house was soon lit up and a thorough search was made. The family living on the bank came to the house to help solve the mystery. Both the room and hall doors stood ajar. There was at the time a few hundred dollars in the book-case which was undisturbed. But surely some mischief was intended. Both families held a genuine watch-night. Only Kittie and her cat were asleep regardless of the watchers. The day following the father and mother and Kittie were in the room. The door was shut. They were talking over what had transpired the previous night when the same rattling of the latch began, the door opened and in came Miss Wooly. Kittie snatched her up in her arms, saying: "Papa, Wooly tan open every door in the house." The father said to her: "Take Wooly and put her out of the back door and shut it." Kittie did as she was bid, put Wooly out and shut both doors. In a few minutes the latch of the hall door commenced rattling, and then the room door-latch, and in came Wooly purring around Kittie. "Well," said the father, "there is your burglar." Mother said: "We must give that cat away." "No, ma, Wooly is mine and you tant give her away taus I go with Wooly." "No," said her father, "they can't take Wooly from you, and you shall have a nice ride to-morrow; Wooly can keep your regiment out at night, and my little lieutenant can command them by day." "Yes, papa, I tan." Kittie had a nice ride the next day. Shortly after this, Kittie was missing again. Her regiment were looking for her, when one of the company saw her on the back piazza rubbing her eyes. As he approached her, he said, "You little runaway, where have you been?" "I taint runaway, I was sleeping." "Sleeping; where were you sleeping?" "Under my bed." "What made you go under your bed?" "Taus the flies tudent bite me." "Now, my little girl, you will be taken to your jail-house." "Tes, Wooly, tan go with me, and papa tan take me riding."

The poor child had become so accustomed to her jail-house that she was sure the penalty would be paying for a ride. She was always cheerful if she could have Wooly to accompany her. She was always questioned by her father when he came home if she had been a good girl. She would tell him all; how she and Wooly were to go to the jail-house, "taus she go sleep under the bed and tudent hear them call."

When Kittie was quite young she was inclined to be religious. She was taught to say her prayers at night, and would almost always remember the text when she came from church. One Sabbath there was communion at the church. Kittie wondered why she was passed by. Very soon three of her little friends came to spend the rest of the day. Kittie went into the cellar, took a bottle of spruce beer and some cake, and said to her little company, "Come with me down to the mill." The oil mill had a large platform. On this she invited her company and said to them, "This is Sunday. We must be good. Now we will have a meeting. Augustus must be the minister and I will pray. Then we will sing 'The New Jerusalem Came Down.' Then Augustus will give us the communion." All this was done with great solemnity. The benediction was: "Lord, keep us. Amen."

We returned to the house. My company stayed to tea, and left for home. "What is the matter with my little girl? She is looking very sober." " I is very good, papa; I took the communion to-day." "What!" "Yes, papa, we all did; Gussie was the minister; I prayed, and we all sung 'New Jerusalem,' and Gussie gave us cake and beer, and we don't play 'it is Sunday.'" "Well, Kitt, I don't know what to do with you." "Send me to school, papa." "It is too far for you to go alone; we shall teach you at home, until you are older." From this time her schooling commenced. Her father would teach her at night, or some member of the family would teach her, until she was six years old. She then went to school.

The early years of school life passed pleasantly, filled with such incidents as a naturally romantic girl usually meets with. I loved my teachers and they seemed fond of me. I remained in school until I was fourteen years old, and had, even though young, noted many things which I shall hereafter speak of.

CHAPTER IV.

"Lead me to mercy's ever-flowing fountain
For thou my shepherd, guard and guide shall be."

At the age of eleven I was awakened under the preaching of Rev. J. Wait, a Methodist clergyman. I was hopefully converted and united with the Reformed Church, of which the Rev. Paul Weidman was pastor. This godly man was installed under very discouraging circumstances. The former pastor was a man wholly unfit for his charge, cruel in his family and very intemperate. The flowing bowl flowed altogether too freely in the house of the shepherd, and too many of his flock followed in his footsteps. Consequently the church had become greatly demoralized. And here I must speak of a rather amusing incident connected with the prevalent intemperance of the church.

Among the farmers living some distance from church it was of course desirable to have dinner as nearly ready on their return home as possible; therefore, whatever preparations could be made before starting for church were usually made. In one family the good housewife had decided upon a dinner of sauerkraut and pork, and as the kraut needed more cooking than the pork the good woman placed the sauerkraut in the kettle and the pork on the table to be added to the boiling mess at the last moment. She also placed on the table, where they would be handy, her little foot-stove, hymn-book and handkerchief. She had also imbibed freely of her *bitters*, as the morning was cold and she must be kept warm; therefore, for her stomach's sake, she had perhaps taken a drop too much. At length her husband drove to the door with the sleigh. She hastened to put the pork in the kettle, wrap the hymn-book in her bandanna, catch up her foot-stove and get into the sleigh. This lady had a fine voice and was one of the leading singers. Arriving at the church she took her accustomed seat conscious of being "all right." The minister prayed and read a hymn. The woman unwrapped her handkerchief to get at her hymn-book, when to her utter surprise, and to the amusement of her nearby companions, she had the pork carefully wrapped and brought to church, while the hymn-book was at

home calmly singing in the kettle with the sauerkraut. Nevertheless this was a highly respectable
woman, a generous, kind-hearted woman, beloved
by her friends and respected by her acquaintances,
the mishap to her hymn-book being due entirely
to the prevailing practice of that day, viz., drinking
rum.

But under the preaching of Mr. Weidman, who
was a wide-awake, God-fearing Christian gentleman,
things began to improve. The indifferent, apa-
thetic, wine-bibbing church members began to
awaken to a true sense of duty. Revival succeeded
revival until what had been but a church dormant
became a church militant. One of the most pow-
erful church awakenings ever felt in Central New
York occurred under the preaching of this earnest
man ; and yet, after a time, this minister, who had
labored so assiduously for this people, and who had
succeeded in building up a church in numbers and
prosperity until it shone a beacon-light to the surrounding Christian world, was brought into trouble
with his church. Mischief-mongers began circu-
lating the statement that he was preaching his old,
sermons over the second time. It was said that
whenever he came to the bottom of his basket he
would begin at the beginning again. This accusa-
tion was absolutely false, as many knew. He did
repeat a sermon on one occasion by special request,
and this was a strong point with his enemies. Disagreeable comments were made against him, he
was not up with the times, was old-fashioned in his

style and opinions, his oratory was not fine enough
to satisfy a certain few who knew as little of true
oratory as they did of Greek, and probably could
not have given any kind of definition of the word
had they been asked. These are the kind of people
who are always the most eager critics. Differences,
disagreements and complications arose until it was
no longer pleasant to minister to this people, and
the pastor severed his connection with his once
loved church and sought other fields of labor, leaving many, however, whose friendship for him and
reverence for his memory will know no end.

Mr. Weidman was my first spiritual teacher. He
it was who first awakened in my young heart the
desire to benefit others, and at the age of twelve
years I was anxious to be a missionary. My pastor
told me I was too young, but gave me a missionary
pamphlet, on the title page of which was the por-
trait of a hideous creature in the form of a woman
in the act of devouring a living infant. She was
called by the natives " Female Devil." As such
they worshipped her as their idol, or their god.
My pastor said, " Kittie would you like to meet
her, and what would you do with her?" "Yes, I
would like to go and kill her." " But we don't send
missionaries to kill the heathen, but to Christianize
and save them." " Yes, but she is the devil and
eats babies, and who ever heard of a Satan being
saved? Mr. Weidman, I would kill her if I could
kill the devil." This ended my first missionary
panic. A latent longing for missionary work has
2

always pervaded my whole life, and now, at the age of three score years and ten, I still think that had I been educated and prepared for the work, it might have proved my most successful field of labor.

But to go back to our church. Pastor after pastor succeeded Mr. Weidman. Their stays being short, little good or satisfaction was gained by their ministries. At length the life of the church began to assert itself. A new church edifice was erected and an eloquent and fearless man was installed its pastor. For several years the church prospered greatly, the minister being popular, and comparative harmony existing. As I said, the minister was a fearless, out-spoken man, and on a Thanksgiving he though it best to point out some of the shortcomings, some of the sins of omission and commission of the infallible four hundred. He gave a plain truthful sermon which probed the recesses of the secret heart, but it sealed his doom. The popular pulse had been touched, a sharp lancet had struck many a vein of pride, vanity and selfishness. The hit aristocratic birds fluttered till their flapping wings created — not only a gentle breeze — but a general cyclone which wafted the incautious pastor to another part of the country.

CHAPTER V.

"Standing with reluctant feet
Where the brook and river meet,
Womanhood and childhood fleet."—*Longfellow*.

But a heavy affliction awaited me. Within three months I lost my father and mother. I had just reached the age of fourteen, and was left homeless. I had acquired a thorough knowledge of the common English branches and had commenced in several of the higher studies, but now the time had come for me to leave school. I must earn my living. O, my, what shall I do? I can cut and make my own dresses, but I dare not undertake to do for others; but I *did* do for others, and in less than two months I had done quite a little work. Just at this time a friend came to me and asked, would I like to teach school? "O, yes, but I am too young. They never have had a lady teacher and of course would want an older teacher." "Well, you are large enough, and they wont ask your age." "Well, if they do, I'll tell them just the truth. But I *would* like to teach." In a few weeks I was called upon for examination before Judge G., Lawyer D. and Dr. P. S. I passed, received my certificate and commenced teaching the first of May. I opened my school by reading a chapter in the New Testament with my scholars, and had prayer.

My school was but two miles from the village, and this gave me an opportunity to continue my studies and recite them to my former teacher, Mr. W., the principal of the academy. My school was quite large, which required more than my lawful hours in teaching. I was very much interested in my school and became much attached to my scholars, and I was in the midst of a church-going community, of Lutherans and Reformers.

They had engaged me only for the summer months, but before the summer months were passed, I was engaged for the winter, and so on, until I had remained with the good people of Stony Brook three years and six months. I had not altogether abandoned my missionary fervor, but commenced home missionary enterprises. There was a class of natives living on the mountain a few miles from my native village. They were a mixture of colored, white and aborigines; were given to drinking fire water, to other bad habits, and were ignorant and illiterate. They were a neglected, despised class of people. Here was a field for home missionary labor.

About this time we had a missionary meeting. A lady came to me to subscribe for another year. I said, "No, Mrs. P., I want every dollar that I can spare for home missionary work." A short time after this I called upon this lady, asking her to let her daughter go with me on the hill to establish a Sabbath-school. "I have already the promise of Mr. K. to go, and if you will let U. go, I will look no further." "Why, no, I can't think of such a thing. It would not be safe for you to go there. It is no place for young girls to go." "Would you let one of your daughters go to Ceylon, or any other foreign mission?" "O, well, that is another thing, a large company go together." "Mrs. P., the Lord will go with me and I'll go." I received a note from a Christian young lady offering her services to go with me. So Miss M. J. Ackerman and Mr. Kingsley and myself took our lunch and off we started on Saturday morning, that being the only day we school-teachers had to ourselves.

We reached the settlement at ten o'clock and visited every cabin and hut, also a few farmers living in the vicinity. We made them acquainted with our business — the object was to establish a Sabbath-school for the benefit of those children who were not able to attend school on account of the distance, and for other reasons. We told them to prepare seats in the grove and the next day at one o'clock we would meet them, and open our first missionary Sabbath-school. After our weary day's work·we returned home. I then called upon a few of our friends to go with us the next day, as teachers, and to take suitable books for those poor children, also for the adults. The next day, after morning service, there was quite a little company of us home missionaries marching up the mountain with a pretty good supply of books. We were all very happy, on reaching the place, to find a large company, varying in age from five to fifty; among the number was a fine-looking colored woman named Mary, who was raised at the South. She seemed to have been living with people of intelli-

gence and refinement. I became very much interested in her as my pupil, and in a short time she
could read in her Testament and was hopefully converted, In the winter season we met at one of the
cabins. The trio was very punctual—neither lost
a Sabbath during the first year. No matter what the
weather was, rain or snow, they too were at their
post. In a little over a year there were between
twenty-five and thirty united with the church. We
had preaching as often as we were able to procure
a minister, and prayer meeting once a week. A
school-house was erected and the log cabins and
huts have disappeared, and many of the children of
the Sabbath-school grew to be respectable, and
married into good families and made good citizens.
It has lost the old name of "Slaughter hill," and the
mountain is now a beautiful farming neighborhood.
The Sabbath-school continued for a number of
years.

My duties and work were too arduous for my
health. I was obliged to relinquish some of them.
I taught school five and a half days in the week,
had a band meeting of young ladies every Sabbath
morning at eight o'clock, attended morning service
and evening prayer meeting. The burden was too
heavy for my age. I had two recitations during the
week. In fact, I found employment for every
hour of my life. My home missionary work is very
dear to me, but that terrible hill of a mile is beginning to make me tired. The rest of the distance I
don't mind.

For nearly two years I have gone that distance, and the Lord has sustained me ; but I must give it up for the present. Others have taken an interest in it, and are doing a good work. My two faithful friends are at the school yet.

I also started a Sabbath-school, for eight o'clock Sunday morning, at my school-house. There were plenty of teachers in this neighborhood. It being the same hour as my band meeting, I could not meet with them.

Shortly after this I had a call to assist in another Sabbath-school on another hill two miles long and two more on the level. I soon dispensed with this ; my help was not necessary. I taught at Stony Brook three years and seven months. A teacher never had better scholars nor a better district. The people were mostly Lutherans and Reformers. There was one Methodist family at the extreme end of the district.

I returned to my native village with the expectation of attending the academy, but the trustees of the village school gave me a call to teach. At this time the third teacher within the year had left the school of eleven scholars. But they thought the influence of a lady teacher would be more successful, and the rude boys be more passive. My brother opposed me, saying, " Kitt, the boys will have you in the creek the first thing, and then what will you do ? " " Take a swim, to be sure. God who calms the boisterous ocean can settle this matter." " Yes, but you must remember that you cannot open that school with prayer." "The Lord will take care of that matter." "Yes, but He will not take care of you in this matter." "I am larger than a sparrow; He takes care of them." I took my Testament and started off to my school, not the least afraid of consequences. I entered the school-room, which was filled to overflowing with students, differing in ages from five to twenty-five. When I opened the door of the school-room, I said, "A happy good morning to you, my young friends. I think we shall have a pleasant school." I asked those who had Testaments to read a chapter with me, and those who felt disposed to kneel should do so, and at the close repeat the Lord's Prayer in concert. So far all my requests were complied with, and but one out of the sixty remained seated during prayer; all knelt save this one. I saw no signs of a swim. I taught from December until the last of April. About this time there were new trustees elected. A lady friend of mine was teaching a small select school in the village, who lost a few scholars by my teaching the public school. The new trustees engaged my lady friend to take the district school, and raised the salary. She, of course, accepted the position, and commenced teaching on a very small scale, only fifteen students. The old trustees, feeling very indignant at the treatment I received, asked me if I would open a select school if they could procure a suitable place. They told me that the whole community felt hurt at the management of the new trustees in this case. I gave my consent to teach a select school. For choice I had rather attend school, for I needed a change, but I did not relish the treatment I received, after putting the school in running order, after it had almost died out of existence.

Two rooms were obtained and were made ready. I commenced my school with fifty-eight students, both rooms well filled. My friend of the public school taught one term and left for want of pupils. I would never allow myself to retaliate, but in this case I felt myself justified. Shortly after, a number of applications were made by her employers for admission of a number of their children. My school was already too large, but I admitted a number of them. Consequently I was offered a large, commodious school-room.

About this time the Court-House was closed against holding religious meetings. The Methodist was the only denomination that occupied the place and of course was ejected. My school-room was large and could accommodate all who attended. I worshipped with them — my views harmonized with theirs on many points. I fully believed in the rights of women to speak and pray in public. My religious sentiments were always found where I could do the most good, and with my Methodist friends I had all the privileges I wished for. But on doctrinal points I was Calvinistic. I had set my face Zionward without looking back. I believe in going on to perfection through the spirit. I never lost my standing or membership in the Reformed church. My name has always remained on the church record. There was at this time a great deal of clashing in the three denominations on doctrinal points. A feeling existed at this time (1842) very different from the present day (1893). The ministers of different denominations now shake hands and preach in each others' pulpits. It must be that the millennium is dawning. The watchmen are seeing eye to eye. Each may retain their own views upon some points. If one believes in the possibility of falling from grace, they would guard against it. If, on the other hand, one believes in the perseverance of the saints and impossibility of falling, all right; let them not look back, with their hands on the plow. I think the fault in most cases is at the beginning a lack of genuine conversion. More of this hereafter.

About the time of my teaching select school, we had a temperance revival, in which I took great interest. One day a little girl came to me with her slate and asked me to write a temperance pledge for her. I said, " Mary, what do you want with a pledge?" " O, we went to play temperance meeting at recess." I wrote something for her in the form of a pledge. I gave the matter no further thought. After this four of my scholars left school. They were always punctual, and very fine children. I must go and see them — they are sick or they would be in school; but before I had time to call I attended a temperance meeting, when a debate took place, and a lawyer of the no temperance side remarked that a certain lady teacher in this village circulated the temperance pledge in school and took the names of the children, without consulting their parents. The father then arose and confirmed what was said. He took the children out of school for playing temperance, for it was nothing else. Children, he said, who are not capable of judging between right and wrong, signing the temperance pledge, and that without consulting their parents! Well, I am sure I never circulated a pledge in school. I dare not rise and defend myself, for it is not proper for a lady to take part in a public debate. But I had just as much as I could do to keep from rising in self-defense. But I wrote my defense and gave it to Mr. T. Lasell to be read at our next meeting.

From this time my temperance work began. I will fight the monster to the death. I asked a Methodist brother to sign the pledge; he said no, for our discipline is pledge enough. Yes, but that will make no difference; the discipline forbids the buying and selling of slaves, but they buy and sell for all that. By having your name to the pledge you may save some one by your influence. He gave me his name. I had good success. My pledge was soon filled. More of this hereafter.

I must give up teaching; I need rest. Seven years have I been teaching with a vacation twice a year of only two weeks each. I close with a full determination to go from home to attend school. Before I was ready there was another call for me to take a school east of the village — this was my old neighborhood. Well, I will teach that school, and then close for a few years. Nothing occurred during this year of much account excepting the death of one of my little scholars. Annie Wood was a very sweet child. I missed her from school. I made inquiry as to the cause of her absence, and learned that she was sick, and wanted to see me. I hastened to her bedside and found her very sick. I said, "Anna, how do you do?" "Very sick, Miss L.; I don't think I can get well; the doctor says so." "Well, Anna, do you want to die?" "Yes, ma'am, the Lord forgave my sins, and I am so happy I want to go to heaven where Jesus is." "Anna, how long have you felt so happy?" "Ever since I first attended school; you talked to the children and then prayed for us, and ever since that first time I have prayed every day, and the Lord made me so happy." "Before you felt so happy, how did you feel?" "Awful bad, every thing that I ever did came up before me; then I prayed to the Lord to forgive me, and then I was so happy." "Well, Anna, would you not like to get well and stay with us?" "Yes, if I could be like you and teach school and pray." "Well, that you could do, should you get well." "Yes, the Lord knows what is best for me. I feel just all the time like I want to go to heaven, and then when you come I will know you, and will you know me, Miss Lawrence?" "Yes, Anna, I shall know little Anna Wood, who came to my school." This was the last day my little scholar

was detained on earth. I called in the evening to
see her. She was passing away. I asked how she
was feeling. "All well, Miss Lawrence; will you
stay with me to-night?" "Yes, Anna, I came to stay
with you." This little Christian disciple of nine
years fell asleep in Jesus that night, to awake to a
glorious morning of joy. She was taken from the
cottage of the poor to a heavenly mansion. I dismissed my school the day of the funeral; had the
scholars in procession from the house to the cemetery, after a brief and affecting discourse by Rev.
P. Snyder. His text was, "Forbid them not, for
such is the kingdom of heaven." I think that children have early impressions, and by proper training would be fit subjects for membership in the
Christian churches, not leave them out in the cold,
exposed to evil influences, until they become hard-
ened in sin. To my knowledge the Methodist
church has taken children into membership as young
as nine years, and they have grown up to be Christian workers.

There was sickness in my father's family and I
was sent for a short time to one of my brothers who
lived in the village. I had heard of Methodism, but
was not allowed to go to their meetings. They had
preaching in the public school-house. Now I
thought I will go and call for one of my schoolmates to go with me. I made one call, but she was
not allowed to go; they told me that they were
very noisy and I must not go, stay here with Anna;
but my curiosity was excited, and of course I went.

There was a small audience. I saw a Mr. B. and his wife, and thought they will be company home for me. After preaching, I waited for them to go, but they tarried for another meeting; there were quite a number stayed and every one arose and spoke. After they had all spoken, the minister came to me and said, "Well, my little girl, do you want religion?" "Yes, sir; I want to be good." He talked very nice and then prayed for me. Mr. K., a political friend of my father, came and spoke to me on the subject of religion, and then knelt in earnest prayer for the daughter of his friend; he also prayed for my father. From that time I became very thoughtful. Previous to this my sister E. purchased me a book. It was the experience of a Green Mountain girl. I read this book with great interest; it made a deep impression on my mind, which, together with this evening's exercises, ended in my conversion after a long and severe struggle.

I had two places for secret prayer. Through the warm weather I had a little bower for prayer near the house; a little grove of small trees shielded me from observation; here I would read my Testament and have my prayer twice a day. In cold weather a small bedroom answered my purpose. Mothers sent their daughters for religious instruction. I attended service at the school-house. The neighbors hearing of it came and told my father that they saw me kneel on the dirty school-house floor, that he must not allow such a thing. But my father knew that his little girl could take care of herself. She was in

good company ; let her alone ; he was acquainted
with a number of those who belonged to that body,
and felt no fears of my going into improper company. But the rest of the family were opposed to
my being a Methodist ; consequently I united with
the Reformed church. The minister, being a Christian gentleman, wished my friends to leave me
alone ; it would not hurt me to hear other denominations, and that I was too young to be persecuted.
This gave me an opportunity to attend other
churches. Dogmatism was not a trait in my
character. I attended Methodist meetings, especially prayer and class meetings, so that I felt myself
a member of both churches. More of this further
on in the near future.

The death of Anna Wood was the only death
that occurred during my eight years' teaching,
which was very remarkable. In my school I had a
miss of fourteen years. She said to me one day,
" Miss L., mother thinks that if I come to your
school one year, and afterward go one year to the
academy, that I'll know enough to teach a summer
school." " You will, if you attend to your studies,"
which she did. Before my year closed, one of my
old employers came to my school-house and asked
me to teach their school, which was a branch of the
" Stony Brook." I said, " No, Mr. R., I shall leave
directly after my school closes, for one year's vacation. I have taught eight years, and I must rest.
But I can provide you a teacher from among my
pupils, if you wish " " That will do, if you think

her capable." "She is capable, but she is young."
"When could I see her?" "Next week; if you call
here, I'll go with you." "Very well; good morning." There on the bench sat my young miss in her
short dress, blue eyes, light hair, and her id
inclining to one side. "Now, my little girl, you
must play the woman. I'll help you." That evening I turned dressmaker. I soon had her ready for
inspection. I accompanied her before the inspect-
ors. She received a satisfactory certificate. On
the day appointed, the trustee called at my school.
He met the young lady, and said, "She looks very
young." "Well," I said, "she is as old as I was
when I taught your school." "Yes, but you were
taller." "Well, she has the brains, and that is more
necessary than height." "Yes, but she don't look
like you." "Well, do you want her?" "Yes, I'll
take her for the summer." She stayed a year.

Soon after my school closed my trunk was packed,
and I was on my way to New York; made a short
visit, and left for New Jersey, where I spent several
months. While in Orange I became acquainted
with an English family, consisting of a gentleman
and his wife, good Christian people, both with
strong, anti-slavery principles. I, of course, for the
first time, became interested in the subject, and
became a willing convert. The last Sabbath of my
stay in Orange was very rainy. Mrs. Kelso and
myself were not able to go to church. Mr. K. was
a class-leader, and of course attended. He said, as
we were not able to attend church, I must write

something for them to remember me by. I commenced poetry. I had never written poetry but once, and then only two or three verses. This was quite lengthy — eight or ten verses. He was quite ｐ ' ·ed with it, being it was composed on the subject of slavery. "How is it, Mr. Kelso, that the discipline forbids the buying and selling of men, women and children, and yet the church allows that very thing?" "Yes, the church South has gone into it, but I think there will be a change in the near future. I think the Lord will take care of that matter." "Well, Mr. K., I hope it will be soon."

In a few days I started for home, Mr. and Mrs. Kelso accompanying me to New York. I came to Albany on the last boat of the season. A heavy snow-storm set in and it was impossible to get to Schoharie, but the word came that the stage went daily from Schenectady to Schoharie. I took the cars to Schenectady, but there was no conveyance between the towns on account of the snow-storm. I remained in town a week. An acquaintance in Ballston heard of my being snow-bound and came after me, and I went to Ballston. By going there, I got rid of teaching for a few months longer. Mr. Jones had a large family of children, and they made it very pleasant for me. I turned governess for the winter — there were six who were old enough for schooling. In the spring the trustees wanted me to teach their public school; I told them that I positively could not, I expected company from New Jersey, and must go to Schoharie. Let your company come here and we will do all we can to make them happy. I consented to teach one term and no more, which I did. A few days after my school closed, I was at one of the neighbors, and little Kittie Jones, my little namesake, came after me to come home in great haste. Some one was there who wanted to see me, but refused to tell who. I returned with her, and to my great surprise, found my dear friends from Orange, New Jersey, Mr. and Mrs. Kelso. Well, they were treated finely. We were taken to Saratoga Springs, Ballston Spa, and made Mr. Mayell an all-day visit. Mr. J. Mayell and Mr. Kelso were great workers in the reforms of those days — temperance and slavery. Mr. Mayell asked me my Christian name. "It is the good old-fashioned name of Catherine." "Well, do you write for a New York paper?" "No, sir, I have never written for any paper." "Well, here it is with your name." "Mr. Kelso, have you done this?" "Yes, for the good of the cause," he said. "And you have had it published without criticism?" "Yes, that was all right."

About this time I had made up my mind to attend school. I went to Saratoga to spend a few days with a friend of mine. While there I became acquainted with a lady who taught fancy-work. My knowledge in this department was quite limited. I at once availed myself of the opportunity, and made myself mistress of the art. My teacher asked me if I could get her a class of ladies at Ballston Spa. I said I'll try. I returned to Ballston and

gathered a large class for her in a few days, also a
boarding place with rooms for teaching. In a short
time the class was in working order. I was her
assistant in teaching, and receiving instruction also.
I had just finished my last course. The lady, Mrs.
Haines, had just received a letter from home, for
her immediate return on account of sickness in her
family. She left the class in my care, and sold me
all the working material. I paid her for the lessons
she had given, and went on with the class. I
finished in a few weeks and made quite a fine profit
after paying for my board and rooms. I had more
money for a month's labor than I would get for
three months' teaching in a district school.

I think I'll follow this work for a time. I understand so many different kinds, if one fails I can take
up another. I may have more money to do good
with. I did so and had all I could do. I followed
this work for a number of years with success. It
brought me in contact with the best of families. I
also traveled considerably. I went to visit a sister
who was living near Auburn, Cayuga county, N. Y.
When I reached Auburn in the evening, it was too
late for the stage. I called on the principal of the
Young Ladies' Seminary, my former pastor in the
Reformed church, in Schoharie. Here I met two
young lady students, and my friends from S., the
Misses E. and the minister's sister, another dear
friend. We had a nice time. One afternoon Mrs.
S. said to the young ladies, "After tea you must
take Miss L. out and show her the city." We were off

in a hurry, going here and there until it was growing late. We were then going through a back street. I said I would like to go to a " Millerite meeting." Just then we came to a church ; we perceived a dim light. I said, " Perhaps it is a Second Advent church." They all said they thought it might be, but none of the party knew. Just then a gentleman came to the door. I said, " Is there service here?" " Yes, madam, walk in." We did walk into a room that would seat about fifty, and to our dismay we were caught in a lively Methodist class-meeting. After the members were through speaking, they called upon Miss E. E. She answered very readily. Next Miss S. She arose and spoke nicely. Now Miss L. I, being accustomed to class-meeting, was at home, but my poor young friend by my side committed herself at once. They had a season of prayer. She was deeply affected. Both the young sisters were converted that night before they retired. Mr. and Mrs. S. instructed and prayed with them, until the burden of their sins was removed. They were church-going people, but these young ladies had never professed religion. Well, we had a good time while together. My brother-in-law came for me, and I left my young friends regretfully. Miss S. and I never met again. O how many of my dear Christian friends have left me to work for the Lord. The messenger must come before long. My visit to Throopsville was rather a singular event. There were two denominations — Baptist and Church of the Disciples. My brother-in-law, an old school Baptist, was constantly urging me to be baptized by immersion. "Yes, but if I should be baptized by a Baptist, I cannot commune with my church; that I can't do; you must let the matter rest." But the matter did not rest. Finally I became acquainted with a few of the members of the Church of the Disciples. I attended their church quite often. I found them Bible Christians; also that they would baptize me by immersion, and I was baptized by immersion without leaving my church. " Well, Kate, you have worked your point very well. I think you would make a good lawyer." "Yes, my good brother, if there was a possibility of my being admitted to the bar, I would commence the study of law at once. The first syllable of my surname is *Law*. If my father had lived, no telling what profession I should have chosen. The Lord knows what is best for us, and if we fully trust in Him, He will direct aright."

Some time after this event, I was visiting two of my old schoolmates, who were members of the Baptist church, excellent Christian ladies. I attended church; we were seated in a side pew — it was communion. When the communicants were asked to take the body pews, they both started. One said to me, "Come, go with us; it is the Lord's table." I did so. After service the minister passed through the crowd, reached over some others, and shook hands with me, saying, "I see you are a Baptist; you communed with us." "Yes, sir; but I am a Presbyterian, and I thought it was the Lord's table."

He bowed and smiled. No doubt he thought it all right. He gave us an excellent sermon before communion.

While I remained at Throopsville I had a severe sickness which reduced my weight considerable. After I was better, there was quite a company of us went to be weighed. Among the number was a Methodist Episcopal clergyman, who was very portly. I was to step on the scale first; my weight was one hundred and sixteen. "Well," he said, "Miss L., vanity is light." "Yes, sir." Now he steps upon the scale; down, down goes the scale, over two hundred. "O, Mr. Wood, sin is heavy." "Yes, you have me now." All this passed off pleasantly. I taught class after class in villages and cities, all that I could possibly do; I had a large school in Geneva; my classes lasted all winter. A most delightful time I had in that lovely town. I attended quite a number of entertainments; at one, dancing was introduced. I refused to join in that amusement, and was asked why I could not dance. "Because I cannot serve the Lord in that exercise. We cannot serve God and Mammon at the same time." And the gentleman that asked me was attending the Theological Seminary at this time. It is so common for people to think that if their names are on the church record, they are safe. We certainly cannot grow in grace and serve the world in conforming to amusements of a nature wherein we cannot glorify God.

Shortly after this there was a call for a directress

in an institution, and some of my friends were anxious to have me take the position. I had no knowledge of what my work would be. We called
on the proprietor, who commenced questioning.
"What has been your calling, Miss L.?" "Teaching." "Do you understand cooking and baking?"
"Why no, sir." "O, I see; you understand Latin
better than baking mince pie." "Yes, sir." A little
merriment followed the examination and we left.
My next class was in the small village of H. I
called at the house of a friend, and asked the old
gentleman how many pupils he had for me. After
he and his good lady inspected my work he looked
at me and said: "Well, can thee darn stockings?"
"Yes, sir." "Well, then, thee can have three of
my girls." "Thank you, friend." I had a fine class.
After this I taught in the village of V. I had my
class in a family where I had the best of enjoyment; it was homelike. Mr. C. had been initiated
into Odd Fellowship the night before. Mrs. C.
and I were teasing him when I heard a tremen-
dous noise of a mother hen and her chickens. I
reached the kitchen first and there was the poor
mother trying to get her little chicks out of the
dough which was standing by the stove for raising.
"O my," I said, "Mr. C., here are a lot of little odd
fellows who want help; come quick and help the
poor old mother hen with her babies." "No," he
said, "that belongs to you ladies. We don't initi-
ate in that way." We had a merry time in extricat-
ing the little mischiefs.

Quite a large company from Cleveland and Painesville, Ohio, sisters and families, came to Mr. C.'s for
a visit. They gave me an urgent invitation to visit
them in Ohio. I promised to visit them the next
summer. The time came, and I went to visit the
Buckeye State. After a visit to Painesville one
of the ladies accompanied me to Cleveland. At Dr.
T.'s we were favored with fine peaches, which we
enjoyed. One day we were to take a ride to Cleveland proper — this was East Cleveland. Mrs. T. and
sister spoke of getting some music, asking me if I
had any choice, " Yes," I answered, " get ' I have
got the blues to-day,' and please let me ask for it."
We reached the store. I said to the clerk, " Have
you got the blues to-day ? " " No, madam, I am
not subject to them," and gave me a queer look. I
asked again, " Have you not got the blues to-
day ? " He was angry. The proprietor came in
his stead. I asked him for a piece of music bearing
that title. He looked over his list but could not
find it. He said he would send for it, which he did.
It became quite popular on account of the joke.
Well, my vacation is drawing to a close, and I now
return to the old Empire State. I like Ohio and
the people. Now I have had a good pleasant rest,
and feel like working again. Back I came and took
up my old business. I have had class after class
until I think a change would be better for me;
perhaps I'll go to school. I started for Cazenovia.
My cousin is steward there, and I liked the school.
I reached the place and thought of attending school

the next term. A lady from New York was getting a class in oil painting. I joined her class and finished one course. About this time the anti-slavery people had an out-door meeting. I did not attend the meeting, but heard a great deal said against it. I thought it very strange that there should be so much said in favor of slavery, where the discipline forbids the buying and selling of men, women and children.

CHAPTER VI.

"Intemperance and slavery; thou two curses of our land."

I at the time took part in the debate, and was a strong disciplinarian. "How is this," said I; "we are not living up to the requirements of the church discipline." Finally I was refused shelter at the seminary. I left the building and stopped with a friend for a short time in the village, who agreed with me on this point, but they were not quite so outspoken. A meeting was called to consider my lack of orthodoxy. I was to appear at an appointed hour. I did not appear, for I well knew that my orthodoxy was all right. After this I attended a Congregational church where intemperance and slavery were preached against as the greatest evils of the present day. I was asked before service commenced to commune with them. I said, "Yes," if one of the deacons and the minister will call upon

the minister and steward of the Methodist Episcopal
church and ask if they knew anything in my Christian character that they could not fellowship.
They firmly replied, " No." What they objected to
was my anti-slavery principles which I was constantly
advocating. This was one of my graduating diplo-
mas. After this I stood alone in the midst of
opposition. I very well knew what difficulties and
persecutions awaited me in my own church. I was
taught that it was a shame for a woman to speak in
public, much more derogatory to her character to
enter a pulpit. I had another hill to climb, longer
and steeper than my " home missionary " hill. But
" Lawrence won't give up the ship ; " it will carry
me safe into port. God and humanity are at the
helm — no looking back; onward is my motto ;
through storm and sunshine the Lord will sustain
me. I know my calling. If I can save one soul
from a drunkard's grave, I shall. be well rewarded.
If half of our church members would direct their
influence against these two great evils, how soon the
victory would be won. But alas, a host is to be
faced of those who once promised before God and
man that they would renounce the devil and all his
works, but at the first election they will go to the
polls and cast their votes for *rum*. What an
example for the coming generation. (They must
be subject to terrible nightmare.) Their party
must be sustained, if it does beggar wives and
children, and fill our county houses with paupers
and our prisons with criminals, and our lunatic

asylums with madmen. If one-half of the evils that are caused by intemperance could be traced to any other source — hydrophobia, for instance — every dog in the land would be killed; mad or not mad, the animal must die; but the demon intemperance is authorized to kill from twenty to one hundred thousand and more, annually, and our laws call him honorable and legalize his profession. O the injustice that is perpetrated, and the curse that falls upon helpless women and children, but more of this hereafter. I continued in my occupation of teaching classes and laid aside my studies for the present. My mind was fixed upon a work in the near future, different from my present calling. The Lord never fails me; He holds me by His power and surrounds me by His mercies. At this time there came an extra call from another direction. A young man was sentenced to be executed at Whitestown in a few weeks. His father had died from grief.

His mother came to me, a stranger, asking if I could do something for her son. His crime was not murder, but arson in the first degree. He was only seventeen years of age. There were three concerned in the matter. One was executed, and one turned State's evidence. It was while this boy prisoner was awaiting the result of the trial of the one who was executed that the mother came to me to do something, if possible, for the life of her son. He was her sole dependence after the death of the father. Learning the condition of the afflicted mother, I set about thinking how to begin my work. As I had had a similar case before, and was successful, I knew very well where to commence. First, a petition must be gotten up, and then the signatures of those who lost property and others of influence in the city of Utica, where the fire originated. A well-known and prominent lawyer was consulted. He gave me my orders and I went to work, praying fervently that the Lord would help me as He always does in a good cause. I was successful. I had no trouble to get his sentence commuted for life. He gave no trouble while in prison ; he soon gave evidence of reformation, and united with the church in prison. Again the same messenger came to me for help. Three years had passed since the boy prisoner had left for Auburn. The sympathy which the people had for his youth and good behavior in prison made it less difficult to get the petition for his release signed. I commenced my work again, called upon the citizens, lawyers, aldermen, and at last and best, upon ex-Governor Seymour, urged him to write a letter to Governor Clark, which would finish up the work at once. He did so, and Lawyer Spencer carried it to Albany, presented it to the Governor, and in a few days returned with the pardon, and the son returned to his mother. He enlisted in the late war and died for his country. I could trace the hand of the Lord through it all.

I continued teaching and talking temperance, occasionally giving a temperance lecture. Now I'll branch out, will go north. In Watertown I had a few acquaintances, and I'll have a vacation and go and see them. I met my old friend and lady teacher, now a Presbyterian clergyman's wife. We had a fine time in calling upon friends. At a new acquaintance of Mrs. S. we met quite a large number of ladies who had come to Watertown to hold a temperance convention. Among these were some of the best talent in the country. A Mrs. Foster from Illinois was there. She was a lady of superior talent, and would entertain an audience for nearly two hours. At this convention I was invited to take part. This was the second time of my entering a pulpit. Two clergymen of my acquaintance were in the audience, from one of whom I was sure I should receive a friendly admonition. The very next day we met, and sure enough he said to me, " Miss L., I bid you God-speed in your work, but excuse me if I ask you to do two things when you lecture, namely, take the altar to speak from, and keep on your bonnet." " Why, Mr. B., the altar is the most sacred place you can put me in. It is at the altar where the sacraments are administered, besides the pulpit is elevated above the audience, which makes it easier for the speaker. We ladies have not quite as strong voices as our brethren. As for my bonnet, God gave me something better for a covering than a bonnet, a glorious covering for the head, always ready whenever I pray or prophecy, as we read in the word of God, I Cor., chap. I, verse 15. Am I right, Mr. B. ? " " O, yes, yes; my wife always addresses the ladies at my revivals after service. She prefers the altar and always keeps on her bonnet, but it certainly makes no difference about those things, the main thing is the amount of good we can do. Miss Lawrence, go on, do all the good you can, no doubt it is your calling. I'll help you all I can," and he did. Mr. B. and a Mr. C., both Presbyterian clergymen, sent out all my notices for Jefferson county. Now my temperance work begins in earnest. I meet with but little opposition, hardly enough to start me in great earnest, but come it will. Let anyone attack the prevailing evils of the land and they will find plenty of work, especially the rum traffic and slavery. The last-mentioned did not occupy quite as much of my time or energies at the first of my public work. In fact the slavery reform had so many able workers in the field that it did not need my help. I had plenty to do in my temperance work for the present at least. I spoke every evening in the week, sometimes twice on the Sabbath — this occurred only when the minister was absent; but by the request of the ministers of the Presbyterian church, I frequently spoke for the third time in the same place. Very often the snowbanks were so bad that it was with difficulty that we could get through. At one time we started to go through a regular blizzard the distance of five miles. We went half the distance, and were under the necessity of returning, and almost perished before we reached home. The cold was intense. The fire was kept up to a great heat at the place of the expected meeting; the church took fire, but was, fortunately, saved by using snow, for they had no water. This was the only appointment that I missed in the county. I was loath to give this up. I never relished a disappointment of this kind. The people of Jefferson county were very favorable to the cause of temperance, and I met with little opposition. With one or two exceptions I was treated with courtesy. My stopping places were mostly in the families of church people, and frequently in the families of clergymen. At Cape Vincent I met with a rebuff in a deacon's family. The madam met me at the door, shut the door after me, and placed a chair as near the door as possible. I saw at once that I was in the wrong place. I said, "Madam, did you not receive a notice from Mr. B. of Watertown?" "Yes," said she, "but I don't believe in a woman's lecturing." "But, madam, do you know where I am to stop for the night?" "I think the Methodist minister will keep you over night." I gave the poor woman a look, and saw that she had a singular expression. I left for the minister's house, where I was nicely entertained. The poor woman got the keys of the church, and no one could get them, but a good place was open for me, and I gave two lectures to crowded houses. There was one place where the notice was not sent. I asked the reason why, and was told that it was not safe for a lady to go there, for two reasons: first, there was no church, and I would be likely to receive eggs and bricks. " Well,

I'll send a notice. They have a school-house, and I'll give them a temperance lecture in that. I can stand eggs, but I don't know about the bricks. I profess to be a reformer, and must take the consequences. I'll go, the Lord will take care of me." The notice was sent — the time arrived. I must go. I reached the place — it was midwinter. Like all "iron works," the snow covered with smoke and soot gave the place a dismal appearance. I called at the house of an elderly couple, who received me pleasantly, but remonstrated against my going to the school-house. Lawrence can't give up the ship now, I thought. No, I can't retreat. They told me a committee of ten would be ready to wait upon me, and take their seats in front of the desk. "Ten gentlemen to wait upon one lady! That is nice, but I have One to wait upon me, and He can take care of the ten."

"Now, my friends, you will go with me; and you, my brother, will open the meeting by prayer. First choose a chairman of one of the ten. He will ask me how my meetings are conducted; and then you pray. Now we will go." We reached the house, which was large and commodious, and was packed. There was one public house, whose proprietor said if I came there he would set me outside. I had no fear of this. The house was for the accommodation of the public. He would make himself liable to the law.

The brother of the hotel-keeper was chosen chairman. The meeting was opened by prayer, and I commenced my evening work of an hour and thirty minutes. The committee of ten walked to the desk and shook hands. The landlord of the hotel and his wife invited me to their house. I said, "Yes, I'll go, if you will allow me to give another temperance lecture, and have as many as can conveniently go to your house." "Yes, all come along," he said ; and then we had another meeting. The proprietor had two sons, lads who were customers at the bar, and were rapidly approaching a fearful end. I heard a year afterward that the landlord sold the hotel and purchased a farm, and was doing well ; and the same year the people had erected a church. My friend, who was so fearful of my being treated to eggs, was most happily disappointed; and, instead of the ten men taking the temperance woman, the one woman gained the victory. So much for trusting in the Lord. Have faith, and He will carry you through.

I continued my temperance work nearly every evening, by forming societies among the young people and children mostly, though some old people joined with us in the work. At this period we were working to get the Maine prohibitory law upon our statute books. A host of ladies were constantly at work all over the State, and, indeed, in many States. Some States had already passed the " Maine law." We had a temperance governor, and our hopes were not to die. The good work went on, and at last came the joyful day. Our legislators did a good work. About this time, hotel-keepers, brewers, and I may as well say the rum power, met in convention. They met at the hotel where I was waiting for the stage. I asked the landlady the object of the gathering. She said that they were taking action against the temperance law, to break it up, because hotel-keepers could not live without selling rum. I opened the room door, thinking I might be able to hear something of their manage-ment that would be available for coming events. Almost the first thing I heard made my blood curdle. It was this: "We must get our heads to work, and make this law unconstitutional." "But," said some, "it will take a pile of money to do that. We must get all the brewers and venders to give liberally. Just think how many hotels, saloons, brewers and a host of others will combine in this business to help us. We already have $40,000 in our treasury, and we can raise $40,000 more. There are plenty of drinkers to help us. Now we shall have to work for it. You see how the women are working for temperance, and even children are being educated in it. Now we must work hard for our rights." "Well, what is to be done first?" One lawyer said, "If we can prove that this temperance movement is unconstitutional, we shall come out all right." "Yes, but it will take a pile of money to do that." "Well, we shall have to pay money if we expect to make money. The lawyers will help us, you know. I tell you the power is with us. The lawyers will carry it to the judges of the Court of Appeals, and they can fix it all right for us. Money can do a great deal, you know. We must work or we will all go to the devil!" O, my! I thought to myself, I wish you were all there now; then you would give this poor earth a little rest. If they knew I was listening and taking notes, I should have to walk, instead of riding in the stage. "The stage, madam." I left, glad to get away from the demon.

Now, Miss L., put on your armor for a fight, an empty purse against $80,000! Only the one strong man is on our side. It cannot be possible that we shall after all be defeated in so good a cause. O, if our churches would wake up on this subject, the rum power could be crushed.

There was another notice sent to a small village for me to lecture on the next Sabbath evening. The hour arrived, I went to the church, there was no one there but the minister and a few members. Just then a gentleman stepped up to me and said, "Don't go in there; your congregation is at the other church; they are waiting for you." I met an appreciative audience, and was informed that the minister of the other church was the proprietor of a small copper mine (head). I met with little opposition during the campaign. The closing up of the Jefferson county campaign was given at the Methodist Episcopal church at Watertown, where I gave the statistics of the county.

A gentleman raised his hand, which was a token to ask a question. I assented. He said, "A certain gentleman living in the county, aged ninety-six, had drank liquor from boyhood and was now enjoying excellent health." "Well," I said, " he became pickled in pure liquor and the adulterated failed to kill him, which might not occur again in a century." My work being finished in Jefferson county, I now passed through part of St. Lawrence county, Lewis county, part of Oneida county, Madison, Onondaga, Cayuga, Seneca, Schoharie, and part of Albany. But the rum power prevailed. The judges of the Court of Appeals were in session at Albany, quite awhile fighting them. There was a tie — four were for sustaining the law and four for sustaining the rum power. One of the judges, who always sustained the law and professed to be a strong advocate for temperance, yielded to temptation and rum was king.

Reader, what do you think became of the rum-sellers' $80,000 or more? Well, if you have a particle of Yankee blood in your veins, you can guess.

After this my lectures were amalgamated with politics and slavery. While I was stopping at Seneca Falls I gave a lecture one evening on temperance. Next morning the door bell rang; I answered, and a stranger asked if I was the lady who gave the lecture last evening. I said I was. "Well," said he, " I am a stranger in this place; came from the East with my family on my way West. Our baby died last night and would you give me money to get a winding-sheet?" " Have you a coffin?" " No, but I can get one." Said I,

" We don't use winding-sheets; give me your name and stopping place, and I'll see that you have a coffin and shroud for your baby." "No, I would rather have the money." "Sir, you are a fraud." He started. I hurried my brother-in-law after him; both entered the bar-room; he had just begun to have a good time. Mr. B. asked him if he was the man who wanted the winding-sheet? The question was answered by his being sent to Waterloo jail, which was the next town from here. A call from a sick family comes next, asking if I would go and see what can be done for them. I go and find a very sick mother and a little daughter of ten years in the same room; two little ones had been carried to their last resting place the day before. I said, " My sick friend, I have come to see what can be done for you." " O," she said, " the lawyer has just been here and given us notice that we must leave here by to-morrow, or he will put us out in the street. If I was only able to be up, but I am so sick and my husband is out of work, and cannot leave us. If we were only in Rochester, he could get work." " Well," I said, " don't you worry; you shall not be put out of this house, unless it is to go into a better one." I got the amount of the house-rent, and enough besides for their present need and started out on my " home mission." I met Mrs. J. A. R. who gave me a good start (she is always at the head of every good work), and by the next morning I had not only raised money enough to pay back rent, but to keep the family until they

were able to help themselves. I met the landlord
in the street the day he was to set the poor helpless
ones in the street. I said, " Stop, sir; I want to see
you on a little business about the family that lives
in your house on the bank." " Well," he said, " I
cannot hear you now." " But you must, or I shall
interfere in a way you won't relish," said I. " What
do you want?" he asked. " To pay you the rent
for that family." " O, yes, yes. Are you a rela-
tive?" " Yes." " How near?" " Ask Adam and
Eve," said I. " Give me a receipt. Good morning." This family was looked after until they were
able to look after themselves.

The ladies of Seneca Falls were workers in the
reforms of the day. Temperance at the present
time was of the greatest importance to them. There
were altogether more liquor shops than the people
felt willing to endure. The ladies met in convention, the subject was agitated, and they came to the
conclusion that a procession should be formed and
a document be read at every hotel and saloon in the
place. This was started, we were treated with
courtesy, and as a result, one hotel-keeper, the best
in the place, retired from the business altogether.
We had one long, hard road to travel — along the
canal, the distance of a mile perhaps. One of the
ladies proposed that two of us take that street to
find how many places there were for selling liquor.
I of course was to do the talking and managing.
We started. The first thing I asked was, " Have you
you any fourth proof brandy." " No," he said,

"but we have whisky." "I don't want that," said I. "O, you want it for medicine, do you?" I think there were eighteen such places, every one had whisky or poor liquor. They all sold the deadly poison, and men, women and children were the victims. It is so strange that our magistrates do not take hold of it in an effectual way. But self-interest blocks up the way of progress in this, as in all other reforms.

Intemperance and politics rule our nation, and politicians work for their party, and the rum party has the money; they can buy votes and make laws to suit themselves.

There are restrictions in the matter of license and officers to carry them out, but how much is done for the good of the people? When a man or woman gets intoxicated, they go to jail — if you can catch them — but the one that caused it goes clear. The one who commits the murder is executed, but the one who stimulates him goes free. There is no doubt but that the greatest number of crimes are committed while under the influence of intoxicants. I have frequently traced them to their origin, and mostly always found this to be the case. One case, a fearful one, was the great fire in Utica. The citizens were, previous to this, in the habit of giving entertainments to the firemen. A few were known to serve stimulants and urge them upon these men. These entertainments were at last known to be the indirect cause of the great fire; showing that the crime had first to be stimulated

by intoxicants; the result of which was, one poor
victim suffered the penalty of the law at Whitestown, by execution, leaving a wife and three small
children, and two aged parents to linger out a life
of sorrow and helplessness; the other suffered the
hardships of a prison and the privation of home and
friends, causing the death of a father through grief.
But money spared the heart sorrows of those who
were the instigators. O, the injustice that is
practised by those in power. Shall not the Judge
of all the earth measure out justice to such? He
said, "As ye do to others so shall it be done unto
you." Life is short at most, too short to neglect
the duties God enjoins upon us, "to do to others as
we wish others to do to us." Time is too short to
let it pass without doing one good deed for our
Maker who has done so much for us. If we were
living in a day of persecution, no one could go into
the reforms without being persecuted. I well
remember hearing of an anti-slavery meeting held
in Utica. Gerrit Smith and son, and Phillips, from
Boston, and numerous others were there, and
were treated to a rain of bricks and eggs, and were
obliged to retreat to Petersborough for safety. I
heard Mr. Smith speak of this at his house. I knew
something of persecution at my time of labor. The
majority of the churches were too quiet. The ministry were right, mostly, but the voting part of the
church was where the trouble lay; their party must
be sustained, reforms were of small account, but the
time will come when we as a nation will be made will-

ing to work by sad experience. At this time the Maine law is dead, the rum shops in full blast, and temperance workers discouraged and almost ready to, and some did give up the ship. But "Lawrence will not give up the ship" until she sails into port. There is something tells me that some terrible event is in the near future ; but I will not give up my work ; I'll take a rest. I went to Moravia to visit a friend who is living in a nice quiet home surrounded by evergreens, just the place for good rest. I reached the desired place and was made very welcome. Now I'll rest both mind and body. All went well for the first week, but before the second week ended a committee gave me a call to give a temperance lecture. I said yes, if they will form a regular temperance organization and work for temperance. This was agreed upon and the lecture was to be given on Sunday evening in the Presbyterian church. Now I shall take a vote before I say a word. If the people are willing to work in the cause, I am willing to help them. The evening came ; the large church, with its deep gallery, was well filled. I asked an expression of the audience. They arose *en masse.* I gave the lecture and gave notice that there would be an opportunity given, on Monday evening, for every one to seal their expression, at the Methodist church. The pastor was present and requested a large attendance. The time came and a satisfactory number became members, of both young and old.

At this time I had another call to go to a neighboring village, and, after a lecture, gather as large a number as possible into an organization. These societies were open to all, except on occasional business meetings. They were composed mostly of young people and children. These are the future of America, and if they can be educated to abide by temperance principles, this nation will be a happy people, for all intelligent and Christian people must admit that rum is the starting point of all the evils of the land. No candid person will deny it. Both of these organizations were worked, both were on the increase and were the opponents of intemperance. Rumors were afloat that our opponents were making ready for a Fourth of July celebration. I said to my people, " Now let us get our armor ready, and have a grand temperance celebration." All consented. The Presbyterian church was open for us, and we commenced work at once. We made fifteen large white banners on white cloth, representing the States that were working for the Maine law. Different mottoes were worked with box-leaves. We also made a beautiful large white banner, with the names of the three judges who were so firm in favor of the Maine law at the session of the Court of Appeals in Albany, worked upon it. Then another was being made at the house of my friend. This was a black monster with the motto " Rum Judges," and their names worked on it. The appointed day was near at hand. We engaged a speaker, the chaplain from Auburn prison, Rev. Mr.

Ives, who was one of the most eloquent speakers of the day.

We had two large divisions. The Moravian order was dressed in blue and white; the other in red and white. Each banner was borne by a gentleman and lady dressed in white, except the bearers of the black banner were dressed in full black. They formed in procession at the church, headed by martial music, and two marshals and other officers of the day. The distance from the church to the grove was nearly a mile, but the day was fine. The distance was almost covered with a temperance army. Two of the deacons of the Presbyterian church were quite opposed to the movement because a woman was the starting point of it all, and they thought it quite out of place for a lady to make herself so public; consequently I had to take up the point and define woman's sphere for two-thirds of an hour. Our exercises were as follows: First, "The Declaration of our American Independence" was read by Mr. Cady. Then singing; then my address, after which Mr. Ives spoke for nearly two hours. Before the exercises were ended, a rush of people was coming by the hundred. "Well," we thought, "can they be disturbers? It surely looks like it; but we must stand our ground. Lawrence won't give up the ship! No, never!"

When our opponents heard of our temperance movement, they put up bills inviting the public to attend a large celebration on the Fourth of July; that there would be a sumptuous dinner served. A great time was anticipated, and all must come. This celebration was but two miles from us, and was intended to break up the temperance movement.

But, to our happy surprise, the rush of people spoken of were coming to our meeting. The ladies of Moravia and surrounding neighboring villages gave a very fine lunch, after the services in the grove, to which we were all invited. We of course accepted, and were served with all the luxuries the season and the country afforded. We then received orders to march back to the church for dismissal. On our way we halted before the first hotel and gave a temperance song, which was not well received. The landlord of the next hotel fell into our ranks, and opened a temperance house. We arrived at the church; and, while giving toasts, the two deacons came to me, giving me Godspeed in my arduous work, hoping that I may live many years to labor in the cause of humanity. I called for an extra toast for the happy conversion of the two deacons to woman's rights. It was granted, the deacons joining in the chorus. We were now dismissed, all having enjoyed a happy day. The battle was ours. We had gained a splendid victory. Although our opponents worked hard to overthrow our temperance movement, they were defeated, and finally came into our ranks. When we live in the discharge of our known duties, we receive help from our divine Master.

A letter came, requesting a lecture on "moral reform." The circumstance was a very sad affair.

It occurred in a near-by village, and aroused the feelings of the whole community. The parties moved in the best of society. A doctor, who stood high in his profession and as a gentleman, the husband of a lady connected with one of the best families in town, and apparently a very happy couple. But the doctor became enamored with a very beautiful young girl, who at the time was a friend and domestic in a family near by. It was thought that both parties might be saved by taking proper measures. The appointment was made for the lecture to take place on Sunday, at two o'clock P. M. We had a fine day and more than a full house: the parties were both present; the lady was placed in the front seat, and during the lecture, I noticed her weeping; it affected me, and it was with difficulty that I could go through with my lecture, although I had my manuscript before me. She once had a mother who cared for her, and now she is cast upon a merciless world, envied by her sex for her beauty, ruined by a demon in human form. Oh, cannot some guardian angel protect and save her! But the poor girl is friendless and alone; her sex deserted her and she fell, and left for parts unknown with her seducer, and the broken-hearted wife left to go to her paternal home. How many could be saved after taking the first step, if mercy and forgiveness were extended to them, and friendliness shown, instead of a cold frown and a haughty look. In such events how many accusers would be able to cast the first stone; but such is life.

Now I am about to return to the place of my
birth. A call for a temperance lecture to be given
at the court-house. A very stormy night awaits me.
I came a little late, but a full house is in readiness.
I commenced speaking in my usual way. When
about midway in my discourse, I was beginning to
remonstrate against the evil habit of drinking, when
a gentleman from the back part of the house started
for the door. As quick as thought I said: "There
is sometimes a making for the door when the nail
is hit in the right place." (An applause.) The man
stood a moment and looked at me. I gave him a
smile of welcome. "Well, I guess I won't go out,"
he said and returned to his seat, accompanied with
another applause. After the lecture, a deacon of
the church of which I was a member arose and said
that Miss L. had come to us like an angel of mercy,
to revive us upon the subject of temperance, of
which there is so much need. Let us appreciate her
labors among us and sustain her sentiments, by
promoting the cause. Schoharie is always ready to
help a good cause. Some of the greatest temperance
revivals have occurred here that I ever knew; also,
some of the greatest religious revivals have taken
place in Schoharie.

I love my old birthplace, every inch of it. No
application for help in the promotion of the cause
of religion, or for deeds of charity, or for whatever
that is just and right but will find a hearty response
in that old county town. It was there that I first
saw the light, and there I shall find my last resting-

place. My thoughts go back to many occurrences of my young days. Shortly before the death of my parents I had on hand a large package of tracts which I purchased from a clergyman. The title of one was "Sabbath Occupation," and another was " An Alarm to Distillers." I thought those tracts might help me in my temperance work. The distillery over on the other street always worked part of the Sabbath. Both tracts are against that, and I must manage some way to have them fall into their hands. At twelve o'clock on Saturday night they stop work and commence again Sunday noon. " Now," I thought, " I'll wait until one o'clock and start out with my tracts." I said to my brother, " I want you to go with me over the field on the other street." " Kitt, what are you going there for ? " " Ask no questions, only go to the fence with me, that is all." I started with my hammer and tacks, left my escort behind, climbed over the fence, crossed the road and reached the door of the distillery. All was quiet within. Now, with hammer and tacks, I fastened both tracts to the door. I heard nothing about them for several days. Some time after, I called at the house of the distiller. His wife said: " Oh, Kitt, did you hear about the tracts that were on our distillery door ? There is one of them, the other is down at uncle's. I have just read it, and I have told our people that they ought not to work on Sunday, they need rest." " Yes," I said ; " besides that, it is wicked to brew and make rum, especially on the Sabbath." " Yes," she said, "and the other tract speaks awful hard about that. I wish I had it, I would let you read it. When they get through with that, I'll let them take this, it is going the rounds, but my husband was awful mad when he found them on the door." "A good sign," I thought; "they may have the desired effect." "They can't think who could have done it. Some one asked Mr. W. and also Dr. V. if either of them had put them there; both said no." "Well," I said, "when you get through with them, let me have them." "Oh, yes, you must read them, certainly." My mirthfulness almost gave me away. But I must not forget my heavenly Father, who was my helper. The establishment was soon after given up. I did not investigate the real cause. It may be that the tracts had something to do in the matter. I think, from circumstances, that was the starting point. At the day of judgment small as well as great matters will be adjusted. Our works will be tried as by fire. If right and good, the fire will purify and they will stand, but, if otherwise, they will perish.

At the age of twelve I went to one of my sisters for a visit. It was about twelve miles from home. While there a company of boys and girls were going berrying; I was asked to go; my niece and a girl friend joined the company and off we started, a happy company. We entered the woods and all were anxious to find the best places. We began to scatter, to see who would be the most successful to find and gather berries. My niece and Angie, my friend, and myself, composed one company. We soon were out of sight and hearing of the others, in a large forest. We walked until we were so tired we could scarcely stand, and we began to fear that we were lost. Shortly we came to a nice spring of water. Oh, how glad we were; now we will have our lunch. After this Angie said, " We are lost; two girls from the same neighborhood were lost last year and remained in the woods until the second night before they were found." I said, " Let us pray the Lord to not leave us in this woods all night." There was weeping and praying for a time. We thought which way shall we go? Angie says, " Let us go back." Rebecca said, " Let us go somewhere." I said, " The way back is so crooked and bad that we cannot find our way out; let us try to find a path or road and keep on that; it will lead us to some house. Now this spring must be visited by something that comes here to drink; I never turn back." " Yes," says Angie, " some wild beasts come here to drink and they will eat us up. You are ready to die, for you are a church member and can pray. Oh dear, what shall I do?" " Give yourself to Jesus, no matter about joining the church now." So we pray again. " Now," I said, " girls, stop crying and let us look around. If we can find tracks then we shall find our way out. Now we must go on; we have been here more than an hour," and on we went again. We began to get weary, but no stopping now. But oh, here is a road, a real road; now we shall get to some house sure. On,

5

on we toiled to reach some habitation. The first we saw was a large field of grain and two log cabins, but not a living soul in them. It was a place where they made shingles for roofing buildings.

We kept on the road ; it certainly would lead us to somewhere. After another long walk through a piece of woods we saw a house, and another a short distance beyond. We asked in the first house who lived in the next. They gave us the name, and I found it was a name that I was acquainted with. I called to ascertain where Mr. Howard lived. The gentleman said, "Come in, girls, you look tired ; have you walked far ?" "Yes, sir ; we got lost in the woods." "Come in," he said, "and get rested." "Oh, no, it is getting late." He pointed out the house, and we hastened on our way rejoicing. We reached the house and were received joyfully. The lady was a sister of my brother's wife. She had us go to bed and rest, while she prepared refreshments for us, which were soon in readiness. After we had partaken of the refreshments, and became a little recruited, we thought of home. "Oh, can't you stay all night ?" "Oh, no, the whole neighborhood will be out with torchlights if we are not there before dark." The horses were soon in readiness, and we were on our way home in good speed. We must have wandered about sixteen miles. The sun is down, and we yet four miles from home. Said my friend, "My horses are great for speed, and don't mind this hilly road."· We soon came in sight of light, when, behold ! There they are at Squire

B.'s already to start for the woods. "Oh, let us shout or we shall miss them." We gave three hearty cheers, and the company answered back with cheers. In a few minutes we were in the midst of shouts and torchlights and not a berry in our baskets. But we had a picnic, and such a greeting. I enjoyed it; my regiment had reappeared, and as there was now no need of their services, soon dispersed. I really enjoyed the woods campaign. I was not troubled about myself, only I was sorry for my two companions. My friend Angie stayed with me that night, and we talked it over and over. I said, "Now, Angie, this had to be so, to bring you to Jesus. You know that there must be a beginning; now you come right out and unite with good people, then when death comes before you as it did in the woods you won't feel as you did then. Sunday evening Mr. Wait will preach, and you must come to hear him. I'll be there, and our friend Jane will be there, and the Lord will take care of us." We fell asleep. The Sabbath came, and the three friends were seated together. After the sermon they had a season of prayer. The minister asked me to pray. We three knelt together, and I prayed fervently for my two friends. The excitement was intense; the one brother and two brothers-in-law came and carried us out, but all ended well. We did not give up. There was will-power with those three children; they were hopefully converted. Oh, I think of the meeting of the many friends on the other side, where there shall be no sorrow, but joy and everlasting happiness. Who would not bear the trials of life, even privation and suffering, for the hope of seeing Jesus, our divine Master, in His glory, face to face? Oh, how much my Saviour has suffered for me, and I have done so little for Him. As the apostle said, " Show me thy faith without thy works and I will show you my faith by my works." I know that I have worked for the good of mankind with an eye to the glory of God, with my heart fully in the work. But oh, how much more I might have done; how many niches I might have filled for the good of souls and the glory of God, but alas, weak human nature fails too often. If all the church members in America or in the United States were living Christians, our land would be a blaze of glory ; there would be a heaven to go to heaven in. But we must lay the axe at the root of the tree, that is the rum-power, the starting point of all evil. It does not look well for a church member to uphold murder, robbery, gambling, houses of ill-fame, profanity, and all the prevailing evils of the day. Oh, no, you say, we abhor and denounce them; but the temperance community are trying to break them up. Where are your votes? You vote for your party regardless of the law of God which forbids your course. You uphold all those things by your votes. Thousands of poor souls are lost, and oh, at the last judgment, where will you stand, when the book is opened and the Judge will say to you, " Depart from Me, ye workers of iniquity." You may be permitted to

say, we are members of the church; we gave money
for missionaries, fed the poor, and so on. "Depart
from Me, ye hypocrites." You have made the poor
with your right hand, by voting to sustain the rum-
power. In consequence you have made wives
homeless, and beggared children; you have filled
prisons with criminals, county-houses with paupers.
Every department in life is visible with misery.
You complain of sleepless nights. No wonder, if
you think of the evils that you have encouraged by
your votes. Your conscience accuses you, and if
your conscience condemns you, beware of the
hardening process that may speedily follow. Justice is coming, and in an hour you think not, may
overtake you. If the righteous scarcely be saved,
where will you appear?

You cannot serve God and Mammon at the same
time. Our brethren tell us that we are going too
fast; we are out of our sphere when we meddle
with politics; the time has not yet come for a prohibitory liquor law, and so on. That has been the
old cry for fifty years, and now the cry has taken
the highest keynote, and we hear the same objection
to-day. The time has come, and we will not give
up our armor until the Judge of all the earth calls
us to our reward. Then let my epitaph be — " She
worked for temperance."

The Woman's Christian Temperance Union has
done wonders, and is marching on to victory. It
has two large political parties to face, and to contend with. But the one God is over all. He con-

trols all parties and unions, and the right will prevail in the end.

Temperance should be a part of our religion. If we read our Bible, as professors of the church of Christ should do, we read that no drunkard can enter the kingdom of heaven. And who is it that makes drunkards? The brewers and the venders. But who is it that gives the rumsellers the authority? Quite a number — the voters, the officers of the law, lawyers and judges, and all who uphold the rum traffic. I was asked if I thought that all those gentlemen were at the head of all the crimes committed in our land? I answered: " Yes; the crimes are committed by authority. I once had an opportunity to look over the records of crime in one of our State prisons, and found that nine-tenths of all the crimes were committed through the influence of rum, directly or indirectly."

The year we had the Maine law upon our statute books made a great difference in the number of criminals, paupers and lunatics. If the present and the coming generation are not educated and thoroughly trained in temperance principles, our nation will become a drunken nation. And upon whom does the great responsibility rest? Upon parents and teachers who have the first care of training the youthful mind. Upon them rests the great responsibility of the future of America — its greatness or its downfall. If your sons are to become great statesmen, let them be taught to fear God and shun evil. Whatever their talent may be, whether for a profession, a statesman or a tradesman, let them have their choice; but let the starting point be right. There is danger on every side. Go through our cities, and wherever you find a public school building, you will find a saloon near it. Often the children go in to get candy. Beware! there is a serpent there watching to coil around them his deadly folds. And are not your daughters in danger of going there? "Not at all," you say. But they are likely to become the wives of the boys who go there. If daughters were taught to shun those who frequent such places, there would be fewer divorces. But how many daughters are being trained in the same direction?

I was asked to give a temperance lecture in a rural neighborhood. There was no church near by, but a fine school-house on the hill, also a deserted hotel. I chose the latter, and the bar for my platform, which some of the ladies trimmed with evergreens. This was indeed the place for a temperance lecture. Oh, how many lost souls have gone from this bar to their final account — the vender with his customers. After the lecture a young man said to me, "I would like to have a debate with you upon the subject of temperance; I can prove from the Bible that it is right to drink intoxicants." "Very well," I said; "do you wish to have seconds, and at what place will you have the debate?" "Oh, at the school-house on the Sabbath, at two o'clock, P. M." "All right; you give general notice." This young man was a law student, not yet admitted to the bar. Well, the day came ; I found the school-house packed, like sardines, and as many more out-side. My friend refused to open the debate. I then arose and commenced the text my oppo. nent had chosen: "Take a little wine for the stomach's sake and thy oft infirmities." I halted for my friend to reply, but the committee failed to get a reply from him, and then I was called upon to give a temperance lecture, which I did. I had a good subject for a beginning, and spoke an hour and fifteen minutes. Thus the expected debate ended. Soon after this, I was called to give a second lecture at Perryville, at two o'clock on a Sabbath afternoon, and one at Canastota in the evening. To do this I had to walk over two miles to Clockville to attend church, where I met friends to take me to Perryville, a distance of five miles, and bring me back to Clockville to give another lecture at five o'clock, providing they would take me back to Canastota for my lecture there at eight o'clock in the evening. This was doing a good day's work — attended morning service, gave a lec-ture at two o'clock, and one at five o'clock, and another at eight o'clock, and traveled fourteen miles. When I trace the past I can see how the Lord sus-tained and watched over me. In all my labors I never failed to meet the best of Christian people. When I gave a previous lecture at Canastota, I stop-ped at the temperance hotel. Mr. Tobey, the pro-prietor, had a cousin preaching in the Reformed church. He called at Mr. Tobey's and said, " I have come to go and hear the lady lecture this evening, for I have never heard a lady lecture. I have just returned from a temperance convention, and feel like going to a temperance meeting."

We halted at the door, and I said, " Mr. C. will you take a seat with me in the pulpit, and open the meeting with prayer?" ".Certainly," he said; " I am not accustomed to wait upon a lady speaker, but I think I can do so." Mr. and Mrs. T. accompanied us at the same time. They, too, thought it rather a new movement for a lady to ask a clergyman to take a seat in the desk. But we are living in an age of improvement. The ladies are taking a step in advance of the times. I hope the day is not far distant when it will not be thought out of place for a woman to go to the polls and vote, irrespective of party affiliations. We are on the march. Rum must yield. God and humanity are for us; but if we have any selfish motive in view, we shall not prevail. If we work for the good of the rising generation, and for the glory of God, who dare say aught against us? Our works will all be tested at the great day of accounts. There are but two ways marked out for us to walk in — the right and the wrong; and it is for us to choose which path we will take ; and if at the end of the race we get poor pay, the fault is our own. A child is punished for disobedience. God's laws demand obedience. If we break His laws we must suffer consequences. Rum and slavery are the prevailing evils of the present day, the latter apparently at a standstill ; the Maine law dead, but not buried. A higher power must permit the galvanic battery to resuscitate both reforms. The one is near at hand, the other more remote. Slavery is confined to a section of the United States, but intemperance spreads over the whole, and indeed over the whole world. The curse is widespread. It takes all classes — the old, and young and middle aged. It goes into every department in life. Ministers have fallen, lawyers, doctors and tradesmen. Thousands are dying yearly from the effects of spurious intoxicants. It kills quickly. Sudden deaths are too frequent to doubt this. It is one kind of suicide, and yet our laws and lawmakers refuse to grant us power to put a stop to this curse. Why, I ask? We can guess the answer. By this craft we have our wealth. There is a wheel within a wheel. The saloon makes drunkards. The insane man, under the rum influence, commits crime ; the lawyer gets his fee. Thus it is that by this craft we get our wealth.

About this time I changed, in part, my occupation, for one that gave me more out-of-door exercise. I took a book agency. In this I could do much good and not dispense with my temperance work altogether. In selecting books I was careful to take those of a moral and religious character. This work gave me healthy exercise and an opportunity to do good to those that I could not otherwise reach. My health and spirits were never better than then. I met with little opposition and that from those who thought that I was out of my sphere. One of my books, " Under God," was the means of converting a Spiritualist to Christ, and he became an exhorter in the Methodist Episcopal church. He was from an excellent Christian family, a professional gentleman, and lived and died in the work of his divine Master. How willing the Lord is to bless our weak efforts when we go to Him in prayer. How He permits our guardian angel to hover around us in all our walks in life, when we work for the good of hnmanity and the glory of God. There are many things that we should guard against in our Christian life. One is spiritual pride. I attended a prayer meeting at the house of my Methodist brother. A clergyman was present; also a very wicked man. The minister asked me to pray, which I did, and it seemed that the very heavens were opened to me. I was inspired with a heavenly influence. I prayed fervently for this man. Considerable was said about my prayers, so that I began to think that I excelled the others, and it gave me a feeling of superiority, and I began to think my Christian friends were not of my standing. I began to feel indifferent, rather cold, but I always read my Bible. In it I found that he that exalteth himself shall be abased. Oh, where am I ? Surely I am wrong. I do not enjoy myself as I once did. I know where to go for aid. The closet there is my bower of prayer. How Satan watches our weak points to lead us from the right path. I was not above being tempted. I must follow the footsteps of my divine Master as far as my weak nature can.

About this time I went to pay a visit to the place of my birth — Schoharie. There I met many old friends and many hearty greetings, as I always do on these occasional visits. One family that I visited lived four miles out of the village. Here the trustees wanted me to teach their school, if only for a short time, as the teacher that had been engaged for the school could not get a certificate, and a qualified teacher must be employed or they could not draw their public money for the coming year. So I went back to my old employment for a short time; had a pleasant time, met old friends that I had not seen for a number of years. This was the fall for the presidential election, and a warm time was anticipated. Three candidates were in the race, Mr. Lincoln, Mr. Douglas and Mr. Breckenridge. Previous to the election, the Teachers' Institute met at the court-house. Professor Holmes presided. A large number of teachers attended and it was a very enjoyable occasion. Soon after this the election battery opened, and the greatest excitement prevailed. Each party was sure of winning. After my school closed, I had quite a good time in attending political speeches, which were very entertaining. Mr. Lincoln was elected. A great torchlight procession in rail-fence form marched from the stone fort of historic fame to the village. Schoharie does work up right when she undertakes. Both parties had very large gatherings. Mr. Douglas was finely represented by his party. But no one thought what the year would bring to our doors. How little we know of the future. It is well that we do not. The time was short from November to April, at which time the commotion commenced in Congress by the withdrawing of Southern members. It was well understood what this meant. As soon as it was reported that Sumter was taken, the ladies began forming societies for the work of preparing lint and bandages, knitting socks, etc., for the wounded soldiers. The next thing the nurses must be getting ready to go to the seat of war. Of course Miss Lawrence must go, for she had nothing to hinder. She will know how to manage. She will go to New York at once, and take lessons in the art of taking care of the wounded. I have almost always felt that I was public property, and now I think I ought to be. I am well adapted to taking care of the sick, but for the wounded I must have more knowledge and experience.

CHAPTER VII.

'Evil oft follows our footsteps,
Do the best that we may try."

Sometimes, in trying to help others, our only reward is trouble for ourselves. We cannot always receive justice in this life. No, we must not look for it. Too frequently we receive a curse instead of a blessing from the very persons whom we endeavor to help.

I was at one time solicited to get up a petition for the pardon of a young man in Auburn prison. He had been convicted of arson in the second degree. After the young man — who was a physician — had been some time in prison circumstances arose which led to the belief that the fire was set by accident and without intent.

After my petition was ready for signatures, I started out. I first called upon the judge who sentenced him. He signed his name with the remark, " He should never have gone there." Next I got the names of the grand jury, then of the lawyers, ministers, doctors and citizens. After a long struggle he was released, and left for parts unknown, thinking, no doubt, that prison birds could succeed best among strangers.

Some time after this I was instructing a class in painting, when a lady, a member of my class, said to me one day, " Miss Lawrence, I have something to tell you after class." The something was this, that somebody — not one of my well-wishing friends probably — had started the report that I had flown away with the prison bird — the young doctor.

" Well," said I, " as I have been here at home and among acquaintances all the time, there has been no chance for me to do much flying."

The slanderer was some craven wretch whom I suppose I had in some way offended, and who only has courage to attack women in some such way. I have no fear of its effects. The slanderer has one exalted quality. He is always reaching up to pull somebody down. They aim at those whom they feel are above them. They seldom attack their own equals. If the slanderer was weighed in the balance, how few scandals would ever get a second hearing.

CHAPTER VIII.

"The flag of our country! we wave it on high,
And swear for her to live or with her to die."

I enlisted as army nurse in 1861 and entered the City Hospital in New York to receive military instruction, such as bandaging and caring for the wounded; as I had already been schooled to take charge of other diseases, I was not long in waiting after I passed in the hospital the required course. A call came from Washington for more nurses. I was one of the number to go. Not a moment was lost. My trunk had already been packed with all necessary clothing. I arrived in Washington at four P. M., put up at a private boarding-house, waiting for Miss Dix's command for business. The next morning when I looked at myself in the mirror I was fearfully frightened, my face being covered with red spots. I rang the bell for the landlady, who came to my aid. "Why!" I said to her, "behold my face, I have no symptoms of the small-pox for I am perfectly well, but what does this mean?" With a smile she answered, "Don't be frightened, they are only the bites of mosquitoes. I forgot to pull down the net last evening." "Well, is that all? I would about as soon meet the bullet, for that would come in my waking hours, but such an attack is mean; there is no heroism in it."

My first initiation into military work commenced the day following my mosquito fright. Miss D. takes me on a visit to several hospitals; one of these had Catholic nurses, Sisters of Charity, considered the best of nurses. After my return to my boarding-house, Miss D. gave me a cup of jelly to carry to the hospital for a sick soldier, and gave me orders not to speak to those Catholic nurses. I thought of this remark on my way to the hospital. "And is this a military order? Am I to lay aside the common courtesy of life because I am to care for the sick and dying? I don't see it. Our soldiers are among the best of the land and so are some of the nurses. That there are some immoral persons among both parties there is no doubt, but to reject persons because they differ from us in their opinion on the subject of religion is not Christlike."

I met those sisters; we bowed and spoke pleasantly to each other. "Well," I said to myself, "I wonder if I have disobeyed military orders. Miss D. is head nurse and is to assign places for the nurses, but she cannot hold office nor vote, therefore, I do not think that I have done wrong, or am guilty of violating military duty." On my return from the hospital my lady led me into a room filled with bedding and underwear, every garment to be put into a pile of the kind. "Well," thought I, "this is queer nursing; my patients are not sick or wounded, and too quiet altogether; I shall become a patient myself at this rate."

But the next day I was requested to get ready for Fortress Monroe. I left Washington for Baltimore with a young German girl about sixteen years old, just over from the Fatherland. I could with difficulty understand her English. Miss D. gave her in my care to make a nurse of her. We took the steamer at six P. M. down the Chesapeake bay, arriving at Fortress Monroe the next morning at six o'clock; we were taken to the hospital, a large building, formerly a boarding-house, containing over two hundred rooms. A room was assigned to me on the ground floor, both dark and damp. The consequence was I took a bad cold. There were healthy rooms not occupied and I must have one. The two German women refused to give me a room. I asked Dr. Smith to look at my room. I thought I took my cold there. Dr. Smith condemned the room altogether as unfit and unhealthy, and gave me a pleasant, healthy room. I had charge of ten rooms. The upright front of the building, a court in the center with trees and flowers and a fountain, and the surrounding waters of the James river and Chesapeake bay, made it a desirable place for the sick and wounded. I had two darkey boys to keep the floors clean, and to do other work or chores. One boy named Billy, who looked to be about

6

seventeen years old, said to me one day, " Misses, you tink I is married?" "Why no, William; you are nothing but a boy." " But I is married to Anna, right-smart yallow gal; you like for to see her, sure." "Yes, Billy; bring her to my room this evening." At six o'clock in came Billy with his "yallow gal," beautiful indeed, large hazel eyes, long heavy eyelashes, features very fine, a modest little beauty — and Billy, a real African — what a contrast. I must keep up a conversation. " How long have you been married, Billy?" "I reckon one year in green corn time." "What minister married you?" "O, Massa married us." "Well, how, Billy?" " He says, ' Billy do you love Anna?' ' Yes, Massa,' and 'Anna, do you love Billy?' ' Yes, sir, Massa.' That is all." " Well, Billy, you are not married. Your wife can leave you at any time. You must be married by a minister; that is, you must be married Yankee fashion."

The next call was from Colonel Johnson and wife, whose business it was to whitewash the rooms of the hospital. They were a fine, portly-looking pair, with European features, almost white. They, like Billy and his wife, were married by their master, and expressed a wish to be married like the Yankees.

The next day the colonel invited me to the quarters to talk to his people; that they would like to live right now, as they had an opportunity to do so. It was Sabbath morning. I finished my hospital duties, and started for the quarters in company with the colonel and his wife. I was surprised to find so large a gathering, over one thousand of those poor, homeless creatures anxiously waiting for something to do. I spoke upon the subject of marriage, referred to the Bible, and now that they were no longer chattels, but responsible people, the Lord required them as such to live as Christians. I took the names of sixty couples and gave them to the chaplains at Fortress Monroe, who performed for them the marriage ceremony.

My stay at this place was unexpectedly short. I was unable to learn what the duties of those two German women were. They were never in the sick wards. They occupied a fine furnished room in the front of the building, and also had good table board. That is all I could learn of them. They were not very friendly toward me, owing to the change from darkness to light. My room was healthy. My bed, chair and trunk were my furniture. I only wished that every poor, sick soldier could be as well cared for. My aim and duty was to care for the sick and wounded, which occupied my time from morning until dark. I understood my business, and was faithful in discharging it. I had a young man from Brooklyn, N. Y., who was taken with hemorrhage of the lungs, who needed close watching and constant care. I went to his room to bid him good-by, saying that Miss Dix came to take me to Baltimore. "I hope you will get well soon." "Oh, no," he said; "you must not leave me now. There is no one here to care for me. Stay, if only a week." The doctor entreated to have me stay, but the old lady was not to be moved. Go I mu.t. Well, this is worse than the mosquito fight. What am I to understand by this? She heeds not the doctor's authority, and yet she wears no military badge. Yet she is to supply the hospitals with nurses, and here the nurse is so much needed, and those ten wards must be left without an experienced nurse. But the doctors are faithful, and do all in their power for our soldiers. In company with Dr. Smith we started for the boat which was to convey us to Baltimore. A regiment of colored people followed us to the boat.

I was very sorry to leave Fortress Monroe. I knew my duty called me there and I was doing a good work; I was treated respectfully by all but the two German women. I was friendly toward them, but they rejected my friendship. I left off trying. I could not stoop to inferiority and left them to their own devices, but I felt a spirit of rebellion when I left. Another such move and I surrender and go on my own responsibility. When we reached Baltimore there were more nurses than wards in the National Hotel Hospital and I was left to work my own way for a short time. A family of friends with whom I became acquainted befriended me. They were in need of a nurse for a month or more. I found one among the ward nurses who answered the call, and I took her ward until her return. On her return I gave back her ward. Soon after this Madam Dix came to Baltimore. We met and I gave her my resignation, saying to her pleasantly that I had always been very fortunate on Independence Day, owing to my independent spirit, and now I'll try it in this case.

"But, Miss L., you can do no such thing, you are altogether in my charge." " Please, Miss D., let me see your credential." " That is not necessary, I have power to retain you or discharge you." " But, Miss D., I have already resigned. You came to Fortress Monroe and took me away from where I was doing a good work, and where the sick needed me, but you heeded no entreaty from doctors nor patients. I came with you to Baltimore. You left me without a ward or even a place to stay. You had the best of recommendations for me from distinguished doctors and clergymen and why you should treat me on such inconsiderate terms I cannot conceive. All I ask is to serve my country in the capacity of a nurse. You gave me no reason for taking me from Fortress Monroe and placing me where I was almost useless only to be persecuted, and now, Miss D., you must relinquish the idea of retaining me as one of your nurses. God bless you, good by."

Now for Washington ; Lawrence must not give up the ship, only with her dying breath, like her distinguished ancestor, the old commodore. I was not long in waiting for a position. Surgeon-General Findley, a friend of a Presbyterian clergyman, received a letter stating that Miss L. was in Washington, would he have the kindness to find her and pro-

cure a seat in a Presbyterian church for her. I applied
to Surgeon-General Findley at once for a position,
which was. granted, as directress of the Kalarama
Hospital. This was indeed a beautiful locality, but
the hospital was an eruptive hospital, with such
cases as small-pox, measles, and other contagious
diseases. My duties were quite numerous but cheerful. My first work in the morning was to go through
the wards and see what was wanting, and have them
kept tidy; also to see that the medicines were properly given, the same being done in the evening. I
had to be cautious in changing my apparel when
going into the small-pox wards. Many of the nurses
were afraid of contagious diseases. I was informed
that they were not obliged to remain more than two
months; then others were to take their places. I
did not approve of this plan for various reasons;
first, there was danger of carrying the disease to
other hospitals; next, they knew how to take care
of their patients, where a change might not be quite
so favorable. But I made no objection to the
present program. The rules were strictly obeyed as
far as possible in this hospital. The head doctor
came once each day. The house doctor was a pious
young man who officiated as chaplain, for there was
no religious service in the hospital, only as we read
the Scriptures and had prayers for the sick and
dying. There was, doubtless, immoral conduct in
this hospital, which manifested itself in strong
terms. A court-martial was called and two of Miss
D.'s nurses were discharged, and a young officer was

sent to his regiment. Miss D. was highly offended by the removal of her nurses and requested the surgeon-general to remove me, stating that she had control of all the nurses. The reply was that he had a recommendation of Miss L. from doctors and clergy from her native city as a competent nurse and a lady. And he also had a recommendation from other responsible sources of Miss L., and that she was now under his charge and directress of the Kalarama Hospital.

Miss D. had those two nurses placed in another hospital, from which they were discharged after the first night. Thus ended the first battle of the Kalarama. This beautiful elevation was the former home of Joel Barlow. At the entrance was a cottage called the Lodge, where the gate-keeper had charge, and also where the laundry work for the hospital was done. This place was surrounded with the beauties of nature. The mansion was a fine, large building, with large, commodious rooms, with marble mantels, and somewhat resembling a Scripture text; not full of dead men's bones, but full of fearful contagious diseases.

We had few officers in the hospital — the head doctor, the house doctor, steward and directress. The steward was an Englishman, and understood his business when sober. He had formerly been discharged for intoxication, but was taken back on his word that he would relinquish the habit and attend to his business. Knowing my temperance principles, he at once manifested a strong antipathy

toward me, although I always treated him courte-
ously as a superior officer. My room was directly
at the head of the stairs, on the second floor. One
evening I came partly down the stairs, and noticing
a number of the soldier boys standing around the
hall stove, I asked them if they would please bring
me a pail of water. Several answered at once,
"Yes, yes." Before they reached the pail the
steward came out into the hall and told the boys
not to go. I said, "Steward, you are out of order;
this is my business, altogether." He gave me an
angry look, and said, "I'll shoot you." "You will?
See here, Johnny, you know that your ancestors
were unmercifully whipped by the Yankees. I will
have some of the same medicine administered to
you." With an angry look he again said, "I'll shoot
you." As he said this, he turned and went back
into the dispensary, as I thought, to get a revolver
to shoot me. I stood waiting long enough to be
shot several times, and then went to my room. He
knew very well that the boys in blue would take
care of him. Besides, the very threatenings he made
would have expelled him in disgrace. I had the
pail of water, and no harm was done. As I went
back to my room I said to myself, "Am I not getting a little rough? Perhaps it is necessary in war
times to be somewhat rough. My Bible says that a
gentle spirit turns away wrath."

The steward had a little stimulant. What a pity.
He comes well recommended and yet he cannot-
leave off the habit of drinking to excess. He is not

exposed to any disease, and why does he not stop
it at once? There should be a sober doctor or
steward to deal out medicine. They may sometime make a sad mistake, and give the wrong th'ng.
Yes, and so it came to pass, Some of the patients
were troubled with sleeplessness after going through
a course of fever. The doctor ordered quieting
powders. One of the young men among the patients
had been studying for the ministry; he enlisted
among the first, was taken sick and was brought to
this hospital, and was considered convalescent, but
like the others was troubled with sleeplessness.
The steward prepared the powders, nine in number,
and served them to the different patients. Before
my bedtime the night nurse came to my room and
summoned me in great haste, saying that young
Wheeler was dying. "What has he taken?"
"Nothing but the powder." "Run quick," I said,
"to the other wards and bring every powder with
you." The house doctor came. He said that
Wheeler must die, as the powder he took was
poison. The other eight powders were brought in
and the men were saved. Had they taken the
powders we would have had nine deaths instead of
one; but this one was too precious to lose through
carelessness. I said, "Doctor, what are you going
to do in this case? The sons of the mothers of our
country are too precious to be laid aside in this
manner."

After the prescription was given by the doctor
the directress' or nurse's duty was to pass them into

the different wards according to direction; but the steward's duty is to see that they are properly made up and given.

One morning I went down into the dispensary for some medicine; the steward was getting ready to go out. He looked up as I came in, and in an unusual manner said to me, "I hope I see you well this morning. You remind me so much of my mother. She was always pleasant and never spoke a cross word. Of course she is quite an old lady now." "Thank you, Steward Abbot, for the compliment. I hope your mother has a son who never gives her heartaches." "Yes," he said, "that is true, but human nature is human nature the world over." "Yes, but when you see a fire must you go and stick your hand into it, or run your head against a post because you cannot conquer your object? The only way is for you to trust in a merciful God." I made up my mind that something new was about to transpire, for such a great change means business, and sure enough the house doctor informed me that the steward had gone to answer for dealing out the wrong medicine, and that he would be court-martialed and perhaps be discharged. A great pity that he cannot get the mastery of his appetite. He has great medical talent, is thoroughly educated for a physician, has the capacity to fill any military or civil department, and yet he will retain his cup and disgrace himself.

"Well," I said, "doctor, will he come back here?" "He may, if they can rely on his word and the court should pardon him." Surely he came back, very gentlemanly and treated every one respectfully. Better times now I hope. I cannot conceive why we cannot be gentlemanly and ladylike in a military hospital as well as in civil life. Surely there is more cause for praying than for profanity, especially among the sick and the dying.

There are daily incidents in a military hospital life that one may think proper to disclose, and one thing is to keep your hands off of that which does not belong to you, of which I shall speak hereafter.

A letter came from an adjutant-general officer from Albany, N. Y., stating that a box had been sent by the ladies at Albany which should have reached me by Christmas, certainly by New Year's, would I answer immediately, telling whether the box had ever come to hand? I wrote that no box had reached me from Albany, but I would ascertain if there was a box at the government storehouse or any other place of deposit. After a long search I found the box at the depot among unclaimed articles nearly three months old. I wondered if it would pay to take the box after so long a time. Yes, I must, and see what is in it. " Yes, send it to the Kalarama Hospital." On it came. "Now, boys, can you get that mammoth box up to my room?" "Yes, indeed we can." When the box was opened I commenced business. Bedding, underwear, choice tea and sugar, dry beef, crackers, all in a good state, but the cakes, which were thrown overboard, four quarts of currant wine, which

can be used, and other articles too numerous to
mention. A short time before this box came I
received one from Guilderland Centre. I wrote
to the ladies to send me some farmers' cheese.
They did so, but it failed to reach me for some
time. This box was sent to the sanitary rooms.
A young man came to see if I was the lawful
owner of a box they had at the rooms. He
said it should have attention, for he thought it
contained old English cheese. I said, " Yes, send
it here." It came, but it was strong enough to take
a fort. It was a good appetizer and the boys were
glad to get it. Also a large quantity of farmers'
sausage that were too rich. These I gave to the
boys and they knew how to dispose of them. The
first night I came to the Kalamara, I lodged in the
room with two of Miss D.'s nurses, who were well
provided for with comfortable beds, while I had
nothing but the bare cot, my only covering being
my shawl, not even possessing a pillow.

Well, I must not give up, but must become accustomed to hardships now that I am in it, and the
room is healthy. I'll live through it and become
accustomed to it after awhile. After a long time
the bedding came from Albany, although I was provided with a room and bed. After the first night
there was no cause of complaint.

Shut in from the outside world among contagious
diseases, my health gave out. I went out Thanksgiving, last fall, and attended church once since I
came here, almost a year ago. I feel sick this morn-

ing. I wonder if I am going to have the small-pox. I cannot go the rounds this morning. The doctor comes in. "What is to pay?" he said. "Well, I believe that I am going to have the small-pox at last." "Well, your symptoms favor it. There will be a breaking out by to-morrow; but should it prove to be the small-pox, you shall have the best of care and a room by yourself, for you are deserving of good care." The morning came, but no small-pox. I was happy once more, as I dreaded the disease above all others, but my health began to fail. Doctor T. sent three bottles to my room, marked "Brandy," "Sherry" and "Bourbon," and gave a strict order to take at least one tablespoonful before going into the ward. Well, I thought it strange that stimulants should prove a preventative at this time, now that I have been here almost a year and escaped so far. I think it folly to take stimulants, now that I have become acclimated, as it were, to the various contagious diseases; I think it quite unnecessary. Besides, I am acquainted with One who takes care of me, who is far better than this kind of medicine. Only a few days ago I witnessed the bad effect of alcohol on a house official. After the fever leaves a patient it is necessary to give stimulants, also in most diseases. The three bottles and the currant wine will find ample use for my boys, who need it. What next? Well, the house doctor and Doctor T. gave me a day off. "Oh, thank you, thank you, doctors! Oh my, where shall I go first! So many places I want to go to. But it will take quite a while to get ready, for I must not carry the small-pox with me." I was not long in getting ready, and started on my day's visit. But when I came to the lodge gate the gate-keeper refused to let me pass. I said, "You must let me out, for I am in a hurry." "Where is your pass?" he said. "I have none; I belong here." A female voice was heard at the door. "Let her out; she belongs up at the house." He passed me. Thanks to the good Lord, He has got me out once more! Now for a visit to some of the hospitals. My first call was at the Patent Office building. The first object that attracted my attention after I entered the hospital department was a young boy about seventeen years old, who at once interested me. I asked him how he was getting along. His reply was "Not very well. I have a bad cough. I can never get well. The doctor thinks my case is a bad one." "Poor boy," I thought; "you would like to get well, would you not?" "Oh, yes, I would, but I see no chance. I am too far gone." "Shall I take your name?" "Yes; my name is Thomas Reese." "Well, Thomas, are you a Chris-tian?" Oh, no, ma'am; no one cares for my soul; no one prays for me." "Perhaps your mother does?" "No, she is dead." "You notice that clock, Thomas; every evening at eight o'clock I will pray for you. Is there anything you would like to eat." "Yes; I think I would relish a piece of cake."

I asked the doctor if he would allow me to bring

THOMAS REESE.

a plain cake into the ward. "Certainly," he said.
I went out quickly and returned with a large sponge
cake, gave my boy friend a good share and divided
the rest among the other patients. Now, I must
leave and go to Georgetown to call on a very dear
friend of mine. She has charge of a large hospital
and of the nurses and is a great worker. I found
her and we had a good time. But she is overworked
and overtaxed, which is the case with many of us
nurses. We are in it and must bear up under it
courageously. The end will come by and by.
" Now, my friend, I must go back to my convent.
Come and see me. Good bye." I hastened back
to my inclosure. The lodge gate opened without
questioning and I reached home very tired. I
wonder how much longer I must stay here. This
day's enjoyment makes me feel uneasy; my health
is certainly giving out. If I die here they must
bury me with the soldiers. Well, that is all right.
Next day one of the cooks died, which made some
change and a little extra work for me. Another
takes her place. One goes and another fills the
place. If ever true Christian American women were
wanted, it is now, in our hospitals with the sick and
dying. We have many such, but we want many
more. The Lord send us the right kind. I wonder
if the surgeon-general ever thinks how long I have
been here. Shut in from the outside world, my
health is failing. Then come those beautiful words:
" Commit thy ways unto the Lord and He will direct
thy path." Then comes a cheering letter from a

dear friend, the wife of the Rev. J. Burchard, D. D., an extract of which I will here give:

"Surely you are now called to bear up the glories of the Lawrence name — a daughter of whom the old commodore need not be ashamed, if from the spirit-land he is now permitted to behold your conflicts, your toils, your faith, your perseverance and your undaunted courage.

'Mr. Burchard unites with me in bidding you Godspeed, also in many, many thanks to the noble Surgeon-General Findley, who stands so high in our estimation, for all the attention and kindness he has bestowed upon you, a stranger in a strange land. We are happy to assure him that his confidence has not been misplaced, *certainly not*, if your heart is as deeply interested in your present mission, as when we witnessed your efforts and untiring labors in the great cause of the 'Maine Question' and temperance movements in this region of country."

Well, I must have had the blues to-day. I will never retain such feelings again; they are wicked. Wherever duty calls or places me, there will I go or stay. Our soldiers are sacrificing their lives to save our government, and I must take care of them when they are sick and wounded. If I die, let me be buried with them; that is all right. I went the rounds as usual, found my duties more pleasant, and became an expert in the symptoms of small-pox and measles, which afterward gave me some amusing incidents in my next hospital work.

One morning, as I started on my mission, the

house doctor informed me that the steward was again in trouble, and in all probability would receive a discharge, if not something worse, if he was guilty of the charges that were brought against him, which proved to be the case. Intemperance was his besetting sin, which led to other crimes, and is the starting point of nine-tenths of all crimes committed throughout the country. It is the reigning king of evil, and yet our laws treat him respectfully. Why not treat him like other criminals, and make an end of him? Oh, because he is so highly connected, he is associated with the best, so-called, and is a welcome guest among the high-lived, and our laws are afraid of him. Our steward, with all his talents and manhood, could not withstand the temptation, and has fallen, poor fellow.

One morning as I was singing, " Jerusalem, my happy home, Oh how I long for Thee. When will my sorrows have an end?" I hear a rap at the door. "Come in." The surgeon-general enters. " Good morning, Miss L., how are you?" "Quite well, sir." "I heard you singing 'When will my sorrows have an end?'" "Yes, sir." "Did you give Dr. B. any encouragement about coming to his hospital, the day you were there?" "No, sir. There was nothing said at all of the kind. All that passed between us that day was, I asked him if I could go out and buy a cake for a sick boy. He gave his consent and that is all I saw of the doctor." "That is all correct. The doctor has made a requisition for you to come to his hospital. It is

for you to say if you would like to go. You have
been a good faithful directress and nurse and it is at
your option whether to go or to stay." "Well, I
would like to go, at least for a time, surgeon-general;
my health is giving out." "Well, whenever you are
ready let me know and I will have you taken down.
Good morning."

"Thy joys when shall I see?" I felt sorry after
all. But sure I am going out. After a while I
may come back. In less than a week a pair of fine
black horses with a fine carriage drove to the door.
I took my exit. When I rode after those black
horses I felt like going to my own funeral. I had
just given good-by to all at the house and was feeling very sober. Perhaps I did wrong in leaving and
I felt that I might regret it. But it is too late. I
must not look back is the great command, and so
on to my new place I go.

I reached the Patent Office and ascended to the
upper floor; was received pleasantly and my ward
assigned me, also the boy Thomas given to my
care. His case was consumption, and with good
medical care and nursing we hoped to see him well;
but in this we were sadly disappointed. At first
we had strong hopes of his recovery. He appeared
to rally, and gave hopes of recovery, but it was of
short duration. A merchant from Utica, N. Y., a
Mr. B., came to see him, and spent the night with
him. At this time Thomas had no occasion to say
that no one cared for his soul. He was ready
whenever the Master called. We had religious serv-

ice in this ward occasionally, and the last night Thomas was permitted to stay with us was a joyful time for him. As was my practice, I called together a few friends to hold a season of prayer and singing. This was attended with great interest, patients from other wards coming also, some of whom shared the benefit of pardoning grace. There was manifested the outpouring of the Spirit of God. I asked Thomas if he had a special hymn he wished to have sung. "Yes," was the reply, "'Nearer, my God, to Thee.'" Looking around, he saw a boy belonging to his regiment, and called him by name and asked him to meet him in heaven. His friend promised, and was much affected. The meeting closed, after bidding Thomas good-night. I then asked permission to watch with him in company with another lady nurse. Permission was granted. About twelve o'clock he said to me, "Turn me over. My father will not be here to see me. Tell him it is all well with me." We turned him over, and before sunrise his spirit departed. I wrote to his father to come at once if he wished to see his son. I asked to retain the body until ten o'clock. I then headed a subscription of my own getting up, went through the building and raised $31. I then went to Dr. Alexander's office and asked him the price for embalming. The answer was, "Fifty dollars." I said, "I have only $31; would you do it for that? He is a soldier boy, doctor." "Yes, I'll attend to him." He came and took the body. I returned to my hospital duties. Another bed was brought in, and a patient to occupy it. Just then one of the lady nurses, accompanied by a gentleman, walked up to my ward. He proved to be the father of Tommy, "My boy is gone," he said. Overcome with grief he could say no more for some time. "Yes, Mr. R.," I said, "but you can see him. He is at the embalmer's. When you get rested I'll have some one go with you." There were a few gentlemen in the building who were always ready to look after such, and this afflicted father was one who was well cared for. After a few days he returned home with his dead son.

A fine appearing lady stranger came walking up to my ward one day, introducing herself as Mrs. W., a member's wife. She asked me if she could do any thing to help me. If so, it would be a great pleasure for her to do so. I said, "Yes. Would you like to write for the soldier boys?" "Oh, yes," she said. After this I had some leisure. She did the writing for the boys and gave them their medicine. This gave me an outing. After a few days a subject presented itself. The doctor had a very sick boy in the convalescent ward. He said, "I think that Patrick will die. There is nothing in the medical line that he can keep down. If you can do anything by nursing I wish you would see to him." "Oh, yes, doctor, if you give him up, I'll raise him," I said humorously. At it I went. Into the kitchen and made a nun soup and then started for my Paddy. There he lay with a woe begone look. "Hello! what now is to pay? Patrick, my boy, and sure you are the one that is to be the husband of one of the nicest Paddy girls in Albany. See here, I promised her a soldier husband and you are the one." I had a merry set around me and Patrick had taken the fourth spoonful of soup. All I dared give him now. "I'll leave you now, but will come again in two hours." As I was passing through the kitchen I met another forlorn looking boy who spoke to me. "Miss L., I guess you don't know me." I said, "No." "I am Eddy C. from Knowersville." "Why, Eddy, how in this world came you here?" I said. "I am a soldier," he said. "What can I do for you, Eddy?" "Give me something good to eat." This was quickly done. The best I could lay my hands on was given to Eddy. His father was a noted physician and I was intimately acquainted with his family. I lost no time in writing to them, and on Sunday morning my letter was answered with Eddy's father, who came after his sick boy.

Well, I must look after my Paddy. I made a cup of tea, a bit of toast and a little dried beef. As I went into the ward several voices called out, "He is better." "Well, Patrick, I brought you a cup of tea and something more to eat. I think you will get well if you are careful." The next morning the doctor went his rounds and returning he halted at my ward and said, "Patrick is going to get well." "Yes, I know it. Now, whenever you have a patient you cannot cure, give him over to me." All this was said pleasantly. The doctor was always pleased

when his patients were doing well, always gentlemanly and never neglected his patients. I had an
enjoyable time here. The nurses were pleasant and
always ready to help each other. There were no
walls between us, as our wards were divided by the
number of beds, thirty being assigned to each nurse.

A young man from New York city was convalescent and had permission to go out one day.
As he passed my ward he said to me, "I am out
to-day." "Well, be careful about eating. You
know how near your roommate came to dying from
overeating." "Yes, I will." And off he went, a
happy boy. In the afternoon he was brought back
in a dying condition. He begged the doctor to be
taken into my ward. "Certainly, bring him in."
In he came, bed and all. He reached out his hand
to me. It was cold. I said, "My poor boy."
"Oh, yes, yes; had I only listened to you, mother.
Oh, may I call you mother, now that I am
dying?" "Yes, all my boys have that privilege." He reached a beautiful glass mug to
me, and said, "Always keep that to remember
your boy." Before this the sun had gone down. It
was sunset also with this beautiful boy. Oh, how
many precious boys have been laid away at Arlington, the beautiful city of the dead. I have often
wished during the war, should I die during this
time, let me be buried with my soldier boys. How
many a poor mother and wife have their loved ones
at the beautiful Arlington. May heaven claim them
at last. We are not always permitted to receive an

answer to prayer in this life, but the reunion in
heaven will tell the story. Another boy is brought
into my ward in a dying condition, altogether
unconscious. Those who brought him in gave me
his name and residence, both of which were familiar
to me. I wrote as usual, but received no answer
until after the boy was dead and buried. A beautiful letter came from Judge D. It was all right, the
boy was already lying in his last resting-place.

One subject of interest after another. One Sunday morning a night nurse came into my ward in
great haste, saying that Sands, our cook, wanted to
see me, he had the small-pox and they were going
to take him to the Kalarama Hospital. I went to
his room, and found him in bed with a comfortable
over his face and that on a very warm day. I
uncovered his face. "Why, Sands, you have the
measles. Your face is covered with them." Just
then in came the head doctor and another doctor, a
visitor. I said, "Doctor, do you call this the small-
pox?" "Certainly I do, nurse." Both agreed upon
small-pox. In came my ward doctor, with another
limb of the profession. All four agreed that it was
a case of small-pox. "I call it a case of measles,"
said I, "four doctors against one nurse. Now, if
this proves to be a case of small-pox you may hang
me sure." "Well," said Dr. B., "if it turns out to
be measles, what then?" "Well, of course, you
four gentlemen must abide by what is right, that is,
you must be hung." All passed off pleasantly, but
Sands must go to the Kalarama. I wrote a note to

the head nurse to have him in a room by himself for he had the measles. I was certain he would be back in a week or two if he took no cold. Lawrence will not give up the ship, neither will she be hung, sure of that, in this case. The symptoms of small-pox and measles are very similar, only different in the breaking out. One who has been familiar with both daily for sometime will see the difference very quick. In this case I was sure and was looking forward to the day when I should have a little amusement with my doctors. The limb of the profession was a Southern gentleman, who took no fancy to the Northern Yankee. He was taken quite sick, now was my time to kill through kindness. What can I do? Well, I will get him a nice breakfast. I spread a nice napkin on a server with toast, and egg, jelly, and a cup of tea, and dry beef. All is ready. " Come, boy, you must carry this for me ; I may not gain admittance." We reached the door and I gave a rap. " Come in." " It is Miss L." " Come in," came on a low key. I opened the door. " Good morning, doctor, I hope to see you better. I thought an unexpected breakfast would relish." I braced him up and placed his breakfast on the table and left the boy with him until he finished his breakfast. Thus the hatchet was buried. Well, what next ? Miss Dix is coming.

I wonder what in this world she is after now. It can't be me I am sure, but up to my ward she came and asked me what she could do for me. I thanked her and said I had need of nothing at present, for

my friends supplied me. She complimented me on
the neatness of my ward and left. She had but
just left the hospital, when, on looking down the
long hall, I saw a man coming up toward my ward.
Well, that is one of the boys of the convalescent
wards; but no, it is Sands. He has recovered very
quick if it is him. Surely it is him. " I am glad to
see you. How do you do ? " " First rate." " Did you
have the measles? " " Yes, I did." " Go to your
ward and we will have a good time to-morrow morning when Dr. B. makes his visits." The next morning
as usual he went through the convalescent ward
first, and on his return he stopped at the head of
my ward. I pretended not to have seen him at
first. I looked up. " Oh, good morning, doctor,
how are your patients? " " Did you know that
Sands is back? " " What, the one who had the
small-pox? You certainly do not mean to say that,
for it takes weeks and weeks to get over the small-
pox." " No, but he had the measles." " What
now ? " I said. " I suppose we will have to be
hung." " Hang four doctors at once? No, we cannot spare them now. The President will grant a
pardon in this case." " I was never more deceived
than in this case. The symptoms are so much
alike."

" Our wards are thinning out. Patrick has gone
to his regiment. I expect the building may be
vacated before long. Then, doctor, I'll have my
furlough. I have not had a rest since I commenced
my hospital labor, and now there is a prospect of

having one." Not many days passed before my anticipations and hopes were blasted. Mr. P., in company with a doctor, came along, who asked me if I would go to a small military hospital on Seventh street, a little out of the city, for a short time. It had been left in a bad condition, destitute of every comfort and without nurse or doctor. That evening I ordered an ambulance, and in company with a lady and gentleman, I made a visit to the little military hospital on Seventh street; but, oh, what a sight! About thirty lying on the floor, on their blankets, so close together that there was not room to walk between them, and many were quite sick.

The other wards were smaller, but in the same condition. Well, I think this place will be my furlough. Surely duty calls me here. This is Saturday evening. To-morrow I can do nothing but see the medical director. I went to the office, but he was absent. Next morning I called at an early hour and acquainted the director with the condition of the hospital. He at once gave me authority to draw thirty men or more if necessary and a requisition for cots, necessary bedding and whatever more was wanting. I hastened to the sanitary rooms, filled my ambulance full of necessary articles and hastened to my field of labor in good season. I had the men carried out of the large ward under the shade-trees, which was pleasing to them, it being a warm day. Some men were set to digging a drain around the building to carry off the stagnant water which stood in puddles. Others were carrying water. Six men and myself were at work in the large ward, getting it ready to put up beds for our boys. A load had already come with one of the best of young doctors. Things began to look quite encouraging. At night our boys had the pleasure of being washed and dressed, with hospital under-wear on, and reposing on clean cots.

A drain dug, the yard cleaned. At this rate my six days' work will be done right. I must here men-tion the kindness of a Mrs. McClellan and a Mrs. Joslin, who were living quite a distance from this place, yet came every day with provisions for the sick. While the New York cavalry were stationed here, another load of ladies drove up, asking what they could do to help. "Oh," I said, "bring a few dishes. We are destitute of those articles. I have made a cupboard and table of dry goods boxes." All came to hand after a short time. The next day we commenced another ward, much less in size and in number of patients. This ward underwent the same round of cleansing. The third day the dis-pensary and some of the smaller rooms were cleansed. This day we had a welcome shower,. which was cleansing indeed. It seemed like a new home, and all were pleased and happy but one young man who I think was homesick, poor boy. What can I do for him? I just had a quilt from the sanitary rooms which had a letter pinned on it, from a young lady, requesting a correspondence should it fall to the lot of a young soldier. Surely this will prove a panacea. I went into the ward

with the quilt. " Well, my boy, how are you to-day?"
"Not very well. I think I must have the blues."
"I can give you a panacea. Will you take it and
follow its directions?" "Oh, yes, madam, but
medicine don't do me much good." "No," I said,
"but here is something that will be beneficial, a
letter from a young lady on this quilt with a request
to hold a correspondence with the gentleman who
receives it. The address is here and is from Buf-
falo." He called for paper and ink. No more blues,
for his mind was occupied.

The fourth day we had a call from the medical
director. "Why," he said, "this is all very nice
and cleanly. Why, this cannot be the place that
was represented to me as being very filthy." "Oh,
yes, sir. It was all of that last Monday morning.
She has had a small regiment to work since then and
we have not got through yet. Please walk into the
kitchen. We are not through with that." He was
told all. "Well," he said, "she deserves a generalship. Where is she?" "Gone to the city after
some things for the kitchen." "Well, she must
have better conveniences than these."

My room was twelve feet long and four feet wide,
with a small window at one end and a door opening
into the hall, or rather something like space. Nothing disturbed me here, except at bedtime when a
regiment of the least little mites of soldiers that were
almost imperceptible were very troublesome. My
generalship would last sometimes for an hour or
more when, weary and sleepy, I would retire,

leaving the dead and wounded to take care of themselves.

My kitchen was furnished at last, consisting of a store, a cupboard made of dry goods boxes, and a table made of the same material.

It was a small military hospital and there was no telling how soon they will have to leave. Therefore, it was not necessary to furnish the building only to make it comfortable for the sick. The young doctor stayed with us only a few days, as he was called to go with his regiment. Another came, a Washington gentleman, so we were left with a good medical department. The two ladies, Mrs. McC. and Mrs. J., were faithful as long as the regiment remained. I was here only a month, and I am happy to say that we had not one death during the month, but we had some very sick men, who were conveyed to other hospitals when the cavalry left.

A lady came to visit her sick son, a little drummer boy. My little room was well filled, but I was glad for her company.

After the excitement of regulating and house-cleaning I was lonely. I will here state that while I was in hospital employment for one month, I never heard an oath nor an improper word. I was treated respectfully and every one was ready to do my bidding and it is wonderful how I held out with all my hard work, both mental and physical, and not one day of real rest or sickness; but plain living and temperate habits with a daily loving trust in my Redeemer helped me. I had long before this graduated in the school of patience and knew very well how to adapt myself to circumstances, and never engaged in any department in life without some previous knowledge of it.

To be courteous is no disadvantage but frequently proves a blessing. "A soft answer turneth away wrath, but grievous words stir up anger."

The cavalry is getting uneasy and wants to be on the move. If they are going to fight, they say, " We want to be at it." Oh, I thought, how many of you will ever be permitted to see your homes! One battle may thin your ranks and leave a small number to return, which proved to be the case with this unfortunate cavalry.

The work of taking down the tents was commenced. The sick were but few, and these were taken to the other hospitals, and soon all were on the march. And now I am sure of a furlough. I went to the house of a friend to get ready to go North. The third day, the lady's brother-in-law gave me a call, and wanted me to go to Armory Square to his hospital, and regulate the wards that were finished. " Will you go?" " Yes, I'll take my furlough there." A new field of duty. " Well, Mrs. S., I have had two days' furlough. I see now that I am government property, so I'll go and see what there is for me to do." Off I went with a little disappointment, but soon forgot it in the work before me. New cots and white spreads, with white fly-nets over the bed frames; and here comes a lot of unbleached pillow-cases. Surely those don't correspond with the white spread and fly-net. So we had them bleached, and all corresponded. In a short time the barracks, eleven in number, were furnished, fifty beds in each barrack, a bath-room, and a room for the nurses. The rooms were nicely finished, with hot and cold water and gas light. It was indeed a fine hospital. I had Ward C appointed me; the boys brought into this ward three small evergreen trees in half barrels, and placed them through the center of the ward. There were twenty-five beds on each side of the center aisle. The gas fixtures were trimmed with tissue paper, which gave a home-like appearance. All things were ready to receive patients, and we were not long kept waiting. The second battle of Bull Run was in anticipation, and not many days elapsed before we heard the booming of cannon. Of course we did not expect to sleep the coming night; that would be utterly impossible. The cooks had all they could do to prepare soup and eatables for our coming boys. At twelve o'clock, midnight, we were ordered to retire. We had time to say our prayers, and then retired ready equipped to answer the bugle call at any moment. Sleep departed, I could not close my eyes. Between one and two o'clock the bugle gave us a call. We were out at our work in a short time ; soldiers were gathering in and around the hospital. Every train brought some sick, but more wounded. The first thing was to give them something to eat, and then the men nurses would take them into the bath-room, and then to their cots.

This lasted over two days. The worst cases were retained, the less serious being sent to other hospitals. Our wards were filled. Mine was an amputating ward. Some of the patients would live but a few hours, and then were carried to their last resting-place. Others would linger a day or more, and then pass away. Others would survive for days, and then leave us.

A company of middle-aged gentlemen came from Boston, and offered their services free. Some came to this hospital. One fortunately came to my ward, and was a great help.

On the afternoon of the second day a young man was brought into my ward. He was fatally wounded, and deathly sick. I quickly brought a wash-bowl. He quickly threw up a reptile about ten inches long. Mr. Cole held him up while I hurried away with it. On my return he asked me what it was. I said, " Nothing unusual." I dared not tell him for fear it would make him worse. He was shot through one of his lungs. Poor boy, how I pitied him! He was so young and handsome. He came from Erie, Pa., and was the son of a widow, and a Christian. Poor mother! a new trial for you. He asked me if he could call me "mother." "Oh, yes; I would like to have you do so." From that time on I was called "mother," and Mr. C. was "father" for all the boys in the ward. Poor young Stratton had one of us by his bedside all the time. This was late in the afternoon, and I began to feel the want of sleep, but could see no way to get any. Miss Dix came to my ward, and said to me, "You must have rest. I'll send you two relief nurses for the night." " Yes, send two elderly, trained nurses." She did so. At eleven o'clock I told them that if he or any one of the others wanted me, to call me at once. I slept soundly, and at one o'clock a rap at the door awakened me. I heard, "The boy is just gone ; he does not know any one ; you had better sleep." But I got up, and went to his bed and spoke softly, " My son, are you asleep ? " He opened his large, hazel eyes and said, " Oh, mother, have you come ? " He took my hand and held it for some time, apparently sleeping quietly until sunrise. He then opened his eyes and said, " Jesus is coming, mother." He then entered upon his last sleep ; and thus passed away a Christian soldier boy.

One of the nurses came to my ward saying, " Miss L., there is a wounded officer just brought into my ward. He says he knows you. Come and see him." " Well, Captain C., how do you do ? " " I am on my back, and I don't know where they will send me." " Well, I have a vacant bed, and you must have it." A stretcher was brought, and the captain was a patient of mine until his wife came to care for him.

A German came in the evening of the sixth day. I said to him, " You had a hard time ; you must be glad that you have reached here after lying out so long." " Oh, yes," he said; "it looks just like heaven here, so pretty and shiny." Poor soldier !

8

the change was so great. My duties are quite numerous. There were ten patients whose wounds I had to dress. The worst cases of the wounded the doctor would attend to. I also tied arteries and administered chloroform.

Another soldier boy had his left arm amputated near his shoulder and was apparently doing well. He was always anxious to have me talk to him upon the subject of religion and gave evidence of a change. We thought his recovery was certain, but all of a sudden his shoulder began to assume a greenish appearance. The doctor pronounced it gangrene. It spread rapidly over his system and poor George was rapidly approaching the end. For the first time I asked him if he was a church member. "No," he said, but his parents were Catholics. "Well, George, would you like to see Father Dominick?" "Yes, I should." I had the priest sent for. Father Dominick came and gave him the sacrament. In a few hours George left us for a better inheritance.

Another patient, a Mr. Smith, expected to be able to join his family in a very short time. His right arm had been amputated. In the evening, before I retired, I called at his cot and asked him how he was getting along. "Oh, first rate," was his reply. "I expect to be with my family in a short time." At daybreak I heard an unusual walking in my ward. As soon as possible I was out in the ward. To my utter astonishment Mr. Smith lay dead. "How is this? Pray tell me." "His arm com-

menced bleeding and we were not able to wake
the doctor and so the poor man bled to death."
"Why did you not call me?" In came the so-called
ward doctor. "Well, there lays your victim;
Reed, .how is that?" "Well, I tried to wake
up one of the other doctors but failed." "You
should have known yourself what to do in such a
case." And so many a one passed away through
unskillful hands. More of this hereafter. The
young doctor left early that morning and no one
could tell where he had gone. Too many experi-
mentalists who were incapable for positions so
important were allowed to occupy places of this
kind. Even among nurses some who had experience and had acquired knowledge of the work were
often set aside and their places filled with inexperi-
enced and ignorant ones through power. I rejoice
that the time has arrived that our American nurses
are being trained for positions so important. A
skillful nurse is as important as a skillful physician. Life has too often been sacrificed by both
professions.

Just now comes a call for me to go to Falls
Church. Another battle has been fought, and hundreds of sick and wounded need care. A lady
comes to take my place until my return. My
ambulance is at the door waiting. On getting in I
told the driver to take me to a grocery. I went to
two of them, and filled my ambulance with all necessary articles of food and luxuries for the sick, not
forgetting palm-leaf fans which were always neces-

sary, and on we hastened to Falls Church. Already our boys were being looked after by a multitude of good Samaritans. All was being done that could possibly be done for them. But we were too near dangerous ground. This was on Saturday, and before Monday our sick and wounded were safe in Washington. The pursuers were after them.

My skill in making wine-whey could not be doubted, but it required pure milk for the purpose, and pure milk for the wounded. The government provided three cows, which were pastured near this hospital, expressly for hospital use. I frequently had some trouble about making wine-whey; the milk was to blame, I am sure; it required nice sweet milk. One morning I got into the wagon with the chore boy, to go on an errand up-town. "Why," I said, "do you peddle milk?" seeing a milk can in the wagon. " No," he said, " I take it to such a place." " But," I said, "that belongs to the hospital. Our soldiers should have that." Sometime after this a lady nurse lingered in my ward for a number of days in succession. After awhile I had a note to call at headquarters. "Well, doctor, what does all this mean?" "It means all this, did you make remarks about government milk?" "I certainly did." "That is enough." "Yes, and more than that; there are jars of fruit in the officers' kitchen with sanitary marks upon them. This I have not mentioned outside. All that I have said was to the chore boy going up to the house, and I say now that our boys should have what belongs to them. I am here to take care of them, and I'll stand for their rights if it costs my head. If you feel justified in discharging me for honesty, all right. Lawrence wont give up the ship."

My old Lawrence ship begins to rise to a warm temperature. " Good morning, doctor," after reaching my ward. I thought I may have a vacation shortly; I need it, so let it come. But here a person tells me that all the nurses are here without pay. I said I was not aware of that, and what benefit would that be to the soldiers.

I have spent most of my money for the boys, and I choose to do so, for then I know where it goes. Thirteen dollars is small pay, and I am honest enough to take care of my own. Well, matters went on as usual for a few days; nothing was said about gratuition. If there were, those who did, have found out long before this who was benefited by their sacrifice. I was aware that injustice was being done, and was fully determined to have no share in it, but was daily waiting for a dismissal. In this I was not mistaken. One morning my envelope came; inclosed was a note that the services of Miss Lawrence would be no longer wanted at this hospital. I gathered up my dry goods and left, fully determined to have a rest of one month. I went to the house of Mrs. S., my old friend, and had a rest of a few weeks. I was glad of the change, which I so much needed. I should now have an opportunity to visit different hospitals. I was aware that another call would come, perhaps too soon,

but rest I must, now at all events. I took the
rounds in visiting hospitals. I called in company
with an officer's wife to visit the old hospital jail, to
see Belle Boyd, who was then a prisoner as a spy.
This was on the Sabbath. We were not permitted
to enter into their apartments as the prisoners were
getting ready to march into the chapel for Sabbath
service, but we were ordered to stand in the hallway
where we could see them as they came down stairs.
Miss Boyd and Mrs. Sprague at once recognized
each other, bowed and smiled, well remembering
when their former acquaintance commenced. Mrs.
Sprague was taken prisoner at the first Bull Run
battle, was very well treated, and there became
acquainted with Miss Belle Boyd, and so the lady
prisoners met under similar circumstances. This
visit to the old Capitol jail was made while I was at
the Armory Square hospital.

A few visits were made to the old convalescent
camp during my short vacation. We would take a
conveyance, and carry sandwiches, cake and other
eatables, for the convalescents, in large quantities.
There would be a number of teams going daily for
this purpose.

One day, as we were going the rounds of the
encampment, two gentlemen stepped up to me,
shook hands and said, "We are glad to see you
here. There is so much work of the kind that you
are doing, that you must be stationed here for this
work." The colonel was consulted, and my place
fixed at the large brick house. Oh, my! this is the

largest ward I ever had. Between seventeen and
twenty thousand convalescents, and some so very
sick, others don't need care at all. I can soon find
out who will need the most care. Back to the city
I went with speed to get ready for my new field of
work. Packed up my dry goods and other articles
necessary for use.

Off I started with my omnibus and driver. It
was nine miles from Washington, and bad roads.
I reached my new place of labor, consisting of a
large room, with a cook stove, cot, table and two
chairs. I brought a few dishes and cooking utensils
with me. Well, I have nothing to cook. I want
things for the sick, especially outside of the hospital sick.

My ambulance was on hand. I went to Washington early in the morning, called at the government
storehouse, gave them my papers of introduction
and of my business, and then selected all kinds of
farinaceous food, such as cornstarch, arrowroot,
farina and tapioca, a box of condensed milk, tub of
butter, a barrel of dried apples, box of crackers, and
other things too numerous to mention. I had
one government wagonload, and my ambulance
well filled. It was dark before reaching the
encampment.

Just after passing through Alexandria, I had to
go through a pond where the water came up to the
hubs of the wagon. I wish they had a railroad
here, and the encampment was on a level. To have
to go up that steep hill and have quicksands to

encounter is not necessary, when there are better places to choose. Landed at last! Now for a beginning — no, not to-night.

In the morning I commenced my work, for some of the boys looked like living ghosts, hardly able to walk. For some I made toast, for some arrow-root, and prepared condensed milk for others. I have to learn what kind of food to prepare for different patients. The wrong food may do great harm.

I must also have a few orderlies to look up patients outside the hospital tents. I had a table made large enough to accommodate the patients who were able to come to it, and they were quite numerous. Most of them needed farinaceous food.

My orderlies came in good time, ready to help. Some would carry apple sauce to those who needed something of the kind. Another would take a little toast or something of the kind. Poor boys, how much they need a good, comfortable hospital and the best of nursing. If I could, I would have you all better cared for. This is no place for the sick and convalescent in a stormy time. It is not fit for a well person. No wonder the drum beats the dead march. In a hard storm it is almost impossible for them to keep dry. I went out to carry something for a sick soldier and the rain was coming through the tent. I found his bed quite wet. I could do no more than send him a dry comforter. This was not the only case. There were many more in the same condition. My mind was constantly at work to find out by what means I could bring about a better state of things.

When they fall on the battle field, we know that is unavoidable, but after they have done all they could to save the country, and then let die, through neglect, is a state of things I cannot stand. Something shall be done. I'll see the colonel. He appears to be a gentleman of refinement. I am sure he will do the right thing. Here it is almost winter and half of them will die before spring.

One day the colonel called at my rooms. I said, "Well, colonel, do you think of staying on this hill the coming winter?" "Oh, yes, I shall have barracks built that will shelter us. I have a pile of boards on the ground for that purpose." "But, colonel," I said, "there is no water here and it is a terrible place to get to with provisions. You have to go a mile from the foot of the hill to reach the top, and it is terrible for heavy loads. You know I came up with three loads and the horses came very near giving out. They were over an hour coming to the house." After I had gone so far I noticed the colonel did not like what I said. But my mind was made up; if there is any thing in my power to make a move, I shall do it. But I must get some one to help me, for our boys shall not stay here through the winter.

Twice and three times a week I make a trip to Washington for things to make some of our boys comfortable, but a few loads are quickly used up among such a multitude and comparatively few are reached. I lose a day every time I go to Washington. My orderlies do well, but I lose the best part of the day. I'll change my time, I'll go at night and return in the morning. Mr. Kings invited me to make his house my home when I came to Washington. My team was taken to the quarters. In the evening I would take my orders from Col. Ruker and send them to Capt. Knowls for the number of teams I wished the next morning. In the morning immediately after breakfast I would go to the government storehouse, where I would meet my teams and have the wagons loaded, and my omnibus well loaded and all ready to start at an early hour, and arrive at the encampment at twelve and sometimes one o'clock, and by two o'clock we would usually be through giving out food at the rooms, but none were ever turned away later. Some days we would wait upon sixty at the room, frequently more. After the duties of the room were dispensed with, my orderlies would take things to the sick outside of the hospital tents, and frequently I would go myself.

One afternoon on my return I came up to the front door. An officer of the day stationed himself in a defiant manner. What now, I thought. I took a sharp look. "I think I know you, sir," I said. "Yes, and I know you." I shook hands with my old school teacher, Dr. J., from New York, I was more than glad to see an old familiar face and friend once more. I gave him an invitation to take his meals in my room, which he did. One of my orderlies, Deacon G., from Potsdam, and the doctor were soon acquainted. Both were Christian gentlemen, which made this place seem like home. The doctor's stay was short, however, but the deacon remained while the encampment lasted.

I stepped out into the kitchen to borrow a tin pan from the cook who had charge of the doctor's table. As I was passing out, I noticed a man lying near a pile of boards. I called the attention of the guard, and asked him to go to him, and see if he was dead, He said, " I can't leave my beat, you must get one who is off of duty." I called another and we went to the apparently dead man, had him brought into my room, and gave him restoratives. The boys were hard at work with him when the doctor came in ; he thought that it was about over with him, but we gave him Jamaica ginger with a teaspoon. After a while he was restored. We then gave him a warm meal and flannels and sent him to the hospital tent. He fully recovered and frequently called at the room. A short time after this the colonel's wife sent a boy in a similar condition to my room, who had nearly the same treatment, and was taken to a regular hospital. Many of our men had a disease that required vegetable food. One of the officers asked me if I could procure any. " Yes, if they have any on hand in the government storehouse, I can get it." Eating so much salt meat and pork is what brings it on. Now for Washington once more this week. After my day's work was done, my driver came up with my ambulance and two black ponies, for " Uncle Sam's" storehouse. I must state here that I was requested to take the oath of allegiance every time I crossed the long bridge, which I made known to him. He told me to keep one on hand, that would do, and for a while every load was searched before crossing the long bridge. This was military rule and was strictly obeyed, but was not closely observed in my case. After awhile I was allowed to cross the long bridge entirely unmolested, not knowing that a strict watch had been kept for quite a time of my doings, entirely unknown to me. Of this I was informed long afterward, and was happy to learn that so much confidence was placed in me.

Now for my Washington trip. I asked Col. R. for a requisition for government teams, four in number, which was granted. They gave me seventy-five bushels of potatoes and twenty of onions, which made four loads. We were only allowed twenty-five bushels to a load, but they put a barrel of dried apples on one load and a barrel of pickles on another. Each load had a little extra. The last load in our train was managed by a boy driver. We were frequently troubled by lads who were watching for a ride between the long bridge and Alexandria, and who were not the most loyal. This day a company of four asked for a ride. I forbade them taking any one on the loads, but the four, not heeding the driver's remonstrance, got on his load. My driver informed me that they were on the last load. " Stop, then," I said, " and let me off." "But," said the driver, "let me go." "Oh, no, I want no fighting; I'll do the work." I took the driver's long whip and back I went. I said pleasantly, "Boys, get off the load, we have as much as the horses can draw." But they obeyed not. With a commanding tone I said, "Will you compel me to shoot you? I shall, unless you are off this moment." They were off, but the driver's whip was all the revolver I had. It answered every purpose. They were very angry and called me an old Yank, which was evidence on which side of Dixie's line they belonged. After reaching old camp, there was no time for distribution. The next day those who needed vegetables were looked up and supplied. The barrel of pickles was distributed from a tent. Among the rest came a patient with a hospital rig on, after a pickle. "Well, my boy, how is this; dare you eat one?" "Oh, yes, when I heard the word pickle, I jumped off my bed; I thought I might as well die coming after it as to die for the want of it." "Well, here is a large one, don't swallow it and make yourself worse. I'll come around and see you soon." This was the case with most of them; they needed a change, but a great many were not able to get any thing. If they had means they were too weak to walk.

One day I was quite busy getting up dishes for my waiting boys. There were quite a number in the room. Two ladies from Georgetown, mother and daughter, came in, very tired — the latter a colonel's wife. They had been distributing eatables to our soldiers and came in to rest. I made them as comfortable as circumstances would admit, excused myself until my boys were waited upon, and then I would see to them. After a short time I noticed the ladies were feeling quite badly. I wonder what I can do for them. As soon as possible I spoke to them and asked them if they would lie down and rest. Oh, no, we are all right; don't mind us. Two o'clock and we are almost through. In came another new caller, just able to walk, a living skeleton. What is the matter and what can I do for you? Poor boy, some toast, a cup of tea and a bit of wine will put a little life and strength into you. When he left he was feeling much better. After this he was a daily boarder. This was not a solitary case. The ladies were overcome by seeing so many ghostly looking human beings; and they said, "The work you are doing here makes us feel that we are doing nothing." In the evening another call came from the hospital. A patient lay in spasms. The nurse came after me, saying the doctors were all gone, would I do something for him? Certainly, if I can. A hot brick, mustard and Jamaica ginger were soon in readiness, and off we were in a hurry. We had just got through when the doctor came into the tent with a scowl on his face, and when he saw me, he said, "What are you doing here?" "Just what you should have done, doctor." The scowl deepened, and, turning to the nurse, he ordered mustard, etc. "That is what Miss Lawrence has just done." He turns to me with a very pleasant, "Thank you." It was my turn to scowl now. I bade the patient good night and left. "Lawrence wont give up the ship." Mules are hard animals to tame, especially when they go on *two's.* To resent an insult is a virtue. How dare he speak so to me, especially when I was doing his neglected work.

Another comes in with his eyes swollen almost shut. "I could put something hot on your face, but if you go out in the rain you will take cold and make it worse. I'll see if there is room up stairs where the orderlies sleep — yes, there is plenty of room. I made a bed on the floor for the poor boy, for the night. At bedtime my patient came back, saying the cook and the other boys drove him out. "Well," I said, "you sit here. I'll go and see the colonel. Perhaps I had no right to put you there." Off I started, through the rain and darkness, for the colonel's quarters. I told what I had done, and the result. "Well," he said, "I'll see; but how did you find your way here through the darkness?" "Come in," Mrs. B. said. "Oh, no, I am all wet and mud, and must go back. My patient is in my room. I must find a place for him." The colonel went with me, taking a lantern, and we got back nicely. The doctor's cook had no right up stairs, and yet he drove the poor boy out of his bed. The matter was investigated, and those who drove the sick boy from his bed were ordered to put up a tent the next day and lodge in it; they were healthy and strong. A short time

after this occurrence I was summoned to the court-
martial department, to appear at the hour of two
P. M. A gentleman accompanied me to the place,
for it would have taken me hours to have found it.
We reached it at last. On entering the tent, the
affair appeared to me so comical that I could not
suppress my merriment. I said, "Gentlemen, what
is it?" "Well, the complaint is that you borrowed
an article of the cook, and never returned it."
"That is true," said I, "but he told me to keep it
until he called for it; it is a dish-pan. Shall I
return it or have him call for it, and what is my
punishment?" "Go back and have him court-martialed." "No; he got angry with me for his being
sent out into a tent to sleep, because he sent a sick
soldier boy out of his bed when he had no right to
do so, for he (the cook) slept in the kitchen, or
should have done so, and the boy was in another
part of the house." "Well," said they, "he deserves
to be court-martialed." "No, let him go. He is
already punished; drop it, court."

"We hear that you are doing a good work here,
madam, and any thing we can do for you we shall
be most happy to do." "Thank you." Then I said
to myself, "'Lawrence will not give up the ship'
until the soldiers of this encampment have a better
home. The ball is rolling, keep at it, only a little
more time. I'll accomplish all that is necessary, if
Capt. S. only gets my papers ready."

Looking out of my back window, I noticed a man
walking in a tent, doubled over apparently in dis-

tress. I said, "Deacon, let one of the other boys look after that; I want you to go with me for a few minutes; I think there is a sick man." Now, with some flannels, a double gown, hot brick (which we always keep on hand), and hot drops, we went in search of our sick boy, and found him very sick, lying on the ground on a blanket, with scarcely any thing over him. The deacon took charge of him, while I went back and sent down a straw mattress and a dish of nun soup. The boy was over the shakes in a few days, and able to be out. In many cases good nursing was all that was necessary.

In the absence of the doctors I would take a peep into the hospital tents. I have just found a German gentleman, quite ill and near the end of his race. He said he came to this country with the intention of making America his home, and as soon as he could find a place that would answer his purpose, he would send for his family. He was a merchant. When he got here the country was getting ready for war. He enlisted in the Union army, and now, said he, " I must die, and never see my family again." He asked me to remember him in my prayers; he was ready to depart and be with Christ. He was glad that I could speak his native language. I asked him, " Can I procure any thing for your present comfort?" He thought he would like a few grapes or grape wine. I was minus both, but he should have it as soon as possible. He had both the next day, and died the day after. How many a noble man has laid down his life

9

upon the altar of his country, and that to save one of the best governments the world ever saw, and may it never know treachery again within its own borders.

One case after another presents itself. Members of Young Men's Christian Associations visit me occasionally, and leave me citizens' clothing, should we need such. There was but one case that I thought myself justifiable in helping. He was old and rheumatic, utterly unfit for military duty. I asked him if he had his discharge. He said, " No, but I can get it." I told him that I would give him what clothing he needed after he got it. After some time he returned, and said he had his discharge. I gave him what clothing he needed, and he left the encampment. I heard afterward that he did not have his discharge. I then made up my mind not to give out any more citizens' clothing. This appeared to be a justifiable case, but it was not my right to do so.

Well, it is getting near winter; my papers are almost ready. If the colonel finds out what I am doing, he will surely send me out of the encampment ; but if the boys get a better place that will be all right. There can be no worse place than this, and my petition is for a place where the cars can bring provision, and where they can have plenty of water, also a place where the four winds are not likely to blow down their tents. Oh, my, I must be courageous even if I am court-martialed! Here are all my papers made out to order. I have put my hands to the work; now I must go forward, come what may. Lawrence must not give up the ship. My two beautiful black pony mules must be the bearers of this, and off we are for Washington once more. I reached the capital, went to the door of the House of Representatives, called for Congressman Goochs, and gave him my papers. He asked me to come in. I excused myself and was off. It being too late to return to the encampment, I made out my requisition for the next morning, sent the ambulance and driver to the quarters, and went myself to the King House.

A lady from Lewis county, N. Y., wanted to see me. She said a young man, her sister's son, came to Washington, and they had not heard from him since he was at the Armory Square Hospital. I said, "What was his business while he was at this hospital?" She said, "I do not know." "Well," I asked, "what did he do when at home?" "He taught school." "Did he ever study medicine?" "No." "Well, there was a young man by that name who was in my ward, and who called himself 'Doctor R.' He let a man bleed to death because he knew not what to do. He also amputated a man's leg, and kept him on the table until I threatened to report him to head-quarters if he did not take care of the man. He was looking to find a bone. The man was faint from loss of blood, and mangled by unskillful hands long enough to be at rest."

Next day I started with three loads for the encampment, which I reached in safety. A number of carriages were being driven through the encampment and around the building, wherever there was room for them to pass through. Some were out of their carriages, as if they were looking up something. One looks like the gentleman to whom I gave my papers. Ah! that's it — members looking over the grounds. I pray that they will do something for our boys. Half of them will not be left by spring if they remain here. Yes, members are looking over the ground. One is shaking his head, another is making his arms go so earnestly. I must not let them see me peeping out the window. The colonel must be out by this time. The doctors are out by two P. M., for the row of patients has disappeared. It seems strange to have them shut the door at two o'clock, when so many have to turn back to their tents, and are so very sick. That poor, sick boy who was brought in here the other day fell down by the door just as it was shut almost in his face. "Well, deacon, why did you not tell me of that at the time?" "Well, you were busy."

It is wonderful how I hold out. I never felt more like working. It must be that this upland is healthy.

Time goes on as usual. Almost a week since this place was under inspection. But they must have some time to select a place and get it in suitable condition. My every-day work goes on as usual.

A week and more has passed and here comes Colonel B. and another gentleman. They both look

angry, passing the window. A rap at the door.
"Come in." "Good morning." "Good morning,
colonel." "Miss Lawrence, I want you to vacate this
room." "To-day, colonel?" "Yes, to-day." "Very
well. What shall I do with the provisions?" "You
can have a tent." A tent was put up for the provisions. "So you want the stove taken down?"
(Oh, he is gone!) In comes the deacon. "Well,
Deacon Goodrich, where are the boys? The colonel
was just in here and gave orders to have this
room vacated to-day. It is early, but we had better
let the boys come and have their rations, and deal
out that which is cooked. They will know what to
do with it."

After the meals were served the rest of the provisions were given to those who needed them. The
stove, mattresses and every thing that the boys
wanted were made use of. There were some sor-
rowful faces to be seen. One poor boy, almost a
cripple, felt so bad, he said he had just begun to get
better; now he would have no one to see to him.
I said the deacon would see to him, and I should
see him occasionally. Thus the day is passing away.
I gathered up my things and had them put on the
ambulance, ready for a start to Alexandria, to stay
a few days before going to Fairfax.

Saturday afternoon I called at Dr. B.'s office.
While waiting my turn, a very tired looking
woman came and asked the doctor if he could
tell her where she could find her son. She and a
friend of hers had just returned from Harper's

Ferry. Her friend had found her dead son and had gone home, but she thought her son was living, and was told that she might find him at the convalescent camp near Alexandria. The doctor, pointing to me, said, "That lady can tell you about that place." I invited her to my room and had her lie down to rest while I was getting tea. After our meal I asked her if she would like to go to the encampment. "Oh, yes." I ordered my ambu-lance and sent a nurse with her. "Now," I said "go directly to Colonel B.'s quarters, and he can tell you if your son is there in a very few minutes. There will be no trouble to find him if you do as I tell you."

Back they came — the poor mother, in her great anxiety, went hunting for her son. "What shall I do?" "Do as I tell you, and you will certainly find your boy if he is there."

She went up again next morning and found the colonel's quarters, but her son was not there; she came back almost heart-broken, and was sure she would never see her son again. "Now, Mrs. S.," I said, "you are welcome to stay with me and get rested, and to-morrow morning I'll take you to Washington and find your son. Now, cheer up. How much of a family have you?" "I have two daughters and this one son. My husband is dead." "How old is your son?" "Eighteen years." "Quite young for a soldier." Monday morning we were on our way to Washington. I went directly to the medical director's office, and found his name.

He is sick at Mount Pleasant Hospital, or the convalescent camp, quite a little distance from the hospital. "Here we are. Now, Mrs. S., you stay here and I'll find in a few minutes if he is here." I went into the doctor's office, and found his name recorded. I asked the doctor to let me go in the ward and see him. I walked through the ward and came to his cot. He was eating his dinner. "Well, my boy, you are doing well, I see." "Yes," he said. I walked around the ward and then came back where he was. I said, "You are quite young for a soldier. Are your parents living?" "Yes, my mother is. I have two sisters, that is all." "Would you like to see your mother?" "Oh, yes; is she here?" "Yes, she is on her way here, but you must not be excited or you may get worse." "No, I wont." "I'll bring her in." After consulting the doctor I went to tell Mrs. S. that her son was here. "But be calm, he is weak, and it may make him worse." But I might as well command the Potomac to run over the Arlington hills. The mother and her boy were clapsed in each other's arms weeping for joy, thanking the Lord that they are permitted to see each other alive. I thought I should come in next for a pressure, but I came off nicely. She then says, "Could you find me a cheap boarding place for a short time, until my son gets stronger; perhaps they will let me take him home." "I'll see the doctor." "Yes," he said; "tell the matron to give her a room until her son gets well."

She had her room and board free. I went back

to Alexandria. I met Dr. K. on the street. He said to me, "I have one of your boys in my hospital, quite sick. He would like to see you. I went immediately, and to my surprise found Deacon Goodrich, who was glad to see me. He said he had his discharge, and expected to start for home the next day. He was taken sick soon after I left, and was brought to the hospital. I said, "Do you know that the encampment is to be moved very soon, to within four miles of the long bridge, right near the railroad, in a beautiful grove of evergreens, and plenty of water?" He said, "I was glad when you left, for I was afraid something would befall you. Some of the heads were very angry at you, and said that you were at the bottom of all that trouble. They knew that it meant something when they saw the members' carriages. But I don't think they were at home. It was after the doctors had shut the doors; some, no doubt, saw them, but then it was too late for them to demonstrate." "Well, deacon, what can I do for you?" "Nothing; but if I am well enough to go home to-morrow, will you take me to Washington, to the cars?" "Certainly I will; I will call about nine o'clock, but don't be in any hurry until you are well enough to stand the long journey." Poor man! he little thought when he left his family that he was never to return to them again. The next morning I was ready to go to the hospital. Dr. K. met me at the door, and said, "The deacon has gone to Arlington. He is through with the trials of life."

I wonder how many more of my boys will go the same way ; two of my orderlies out of six are gone. I'll be glad when they are all moved ; they were putting up barracks, I heard, a week ago. I must go and see the place when they all get there.

To-morrow I go to Fairfax ; there I go in a regular hospital ; that will be nice. The morning comes, and I start for my new quarters, and passed the old encampment. It looks as usual, a city of tents, white sepulchers, full of living bones. Never mind, you will have a better home very soon. Your cottages are peeping through the evergreens. They will soon be ready to receive you.

I have reached my new home all right. I commence at once to unload and make myself at home in regulating my room. I feel very tired and must rest. To-morrow I'll take care of the sick. The next day found me very busy in waiting upon the sick. The wards are not crowded, but some quite sick. All things went on in usual hospital style. Some were convalescent, some quite sick, and others ready to go to their regiment. One morning I sent for my driver to get ready for Washington. I wanted things for the boys. My pony mules were in fine order. As we were nearing the old encampment the driver called out, "Oh, Miss, look out ! Why a regiment is coming !" Said I, "No, a brigade — two or three brigades, but they are all coming this way, and we shall meet them. We must turn out." " No," he said, " they are going to the right ; drive on, I want to see them." Coming nearer, who should it be but the brave boys of the old encampment, marching across the hill to their new home. My driver and ponies were soon noticed, and such a noise and shout went up—

Lawrence wont give up the ship." I waved my handkerchief, all the time crying like a baby. The battle was won. Those who were able to go on foot marched across, the distance being shorter. They carried all they could with them, such as camp-kettles and blankets, etc. I met loads further on. If ever I thanked my Heavenly Father sincerely, it was this day. I went on my way rejoicing to think that I had done a little good. That old convalescent camp was a place of human sacrifice for man and beasts also. The drum could be heard beating the dead march at any time. Now it will be different. Every thing they need can reach them by railroad, and they have plenty of water in a valley among evergreens, and in their barracks they are sheltered from cold and rain. God bless our boys! They have saved our country by Thy help.

On reaching Washington I was put on the committee for getting ready Christmas dinners for our soldiers. I was on the committee for convalescent camp. I said to Mrs. K., " I'll help on Christmas day, but I cannot leave my hospital work to help cook and bake. I would be glad to help if I were near you, but I'll come down the day before, and do all I can on Christmas day." Back to my hospital work. Nothing of much account occurs between this and my coming engagement. A woman came to my room one day and asked me for some provisions. I of course inquired into her circumstances. She said she was left with a family of small children. "Have you a husband?" I asked. "Yes, but he is gone." "Is he a soldier?" "Yes." "Well, don't you hear from him?" We looked each other straight in the face. She burst into tears. The story is told. Her husband had gone into the Confederate army, and she and her children were left in a destitute condition.

"My poor sister, don't feel so badly. I'll see to you, but say nothing. Come to me every day." I would take the value of my rations in money, and yet whatever I wished I always had plenty of, beans, rice, farina, cornstarch and the like, on hand, and the grounds are seldom vacant, and whenever a regiment or brigade moved they left plenty of provisions. I can help the poor woman, but I don't really know that I have a right to. I may get a court-martial again. My mind was not quite at rest, but my friend had her rations every day. I should not let her and her helpless children go without food.

My work went on as usual with an occasional interruption. To this I became accustomed. Almost every day brings a new subject. I hope nothing will interfere with my going to-morrow to help serve the Christmas dinner as I have promised.

Now, there are some clothes that must be washed immediately. I went down into the yard, met

Helen, and asked her if she could do some extra washing for me, so that I could have them to-morrow afternoon.

"It is pretty near Christmas," she said, "but I'll do them to-day." "But, Helen, see there, where did that white child come from?" "Well, Missus, they come, a company of them, here a short time ago. The family all died and left the three children to the care of the slaves and were told to go into the Union lines, and that one is the youngest of them. Now, Missus, you had better take her, and not think of taking my little boy, he is my baby and I don't want to part with him." "Oh, no, Helen, I wont take your boy, you have more need of him than I have." "But that little girl has no one to see to her. She will be glad to live with you, and then she is white and more like you white folks, and I'll go with you to the other two girls, if you will take her." "Oh, Helen, not now. I am going away to-morrow, and I have no time now." So I go back to my work wondering if I can leave every thing all right. There are none very sick now. But I must go at all events unless I can save life by staying here. I shall be absent only one night. The next afternoon I reached Washington, went to work and found enough to do.

Christmas day came. We started at an early hour. Most of the provisions were sent by railroad, such as apples, oranges, oysters, and all such as could be sent in barrels and boxes. Turkey and poultry of all kinds, and vegetables, pies, puddings and cakes, were sent in government wagons. A long row of government teams and carriages, headed by the well-known black ponies, were on the way to the new convalescent camp. On our arrival the band struck up "Yankee Doodle." All things went off very nicely. It was the wish of the committee that we all share alike.

I met some old acquaintances from New York State that I was very glad to see. But I did not forget the colonel of the old encampment. A large tin-pan was fitted out with some of all the luxuries we had and forwarded to him.

This was a hard day's labor for the committee, but we enjoyed it, for we knew that the boys had a happy day and that made the burden light.

Weary after my day's work, I returned to my hospital duties. The next day I had a call from Helen, with two little girls, and a sister of the little one that she wanted me to take. "This one you can have as your own," the sister said with a tremor in her voice. "You do not want to give away your sister, do you? I have no home now for myself, nor for her," I said. "I reckon she will be better off with you than with me; I have a sister younger than I am ; I reckon I must look after her some." "You poor child," I thought, "not more than twelve years old yourself, and the care of two children, and no means of support." They were represented to me as slave children. The little girl had flaxen hair and dark blue eyes, but dark complexion, or terribly sunburned. I at once took the child, thinking I would find a home for her. She was a beautiful child, and I soon became very much attached to her. She was not yet three years old. I thought I would keep her until I could find a place for her. I was aware that a hospital was not a proper place, even if I were permitted to keep her with me, but I will keep her here for a short time.

Helen comes. "Missus, there is a wedding to-morrow night, Jacob and Anna to be married. They want you to come, and I have come to give you an invitation. "Where is it?" I asked. "In the chapel." "Yes, I'll come." The chapel was directly under my room. "May I ask Miss Jackson?" "Yes." This was the second wedding that I was invited to attend. There was a large gathering. The groom was a recruiting officer. The bride had always lived in one of the best families of Virginia. There was quite a large number of white people, especially officers, to witness the ceremony. It was performed by Rev. Washburn, an Episcopal clergyman, and was done briefly and in order. After a bountiful repast for the young couple and their especial company they returned to the chapel, where they had music and dancing. We remained to witness a few rounds and retired. Many officers danced with the bride, who was very handsome, and but little darker than a brunette. The husband was darker. They made a fine appearance. He was dressed in his uniform, and the bride in white. Thus passed off the second wedding while in this hospital. But another was in anticipation. I was just thinking how many changes I had passed through since I first came to Washington. Had all the hardship that I have encountered been brought to view at once, I certainly could not have withstood the thought. But upheld by an unseen hand I have been permitted to stand the burdens laid upon me. As one after another came, I had strength given for endurance. The soldiers were always respectful, and were ready to appreciate a kindness, which always paid for kindness bestowed. Aside from any daily work of caring for the sick, I was always ready to work to better the condition of the soldiers, as in the case of the old convalescent camp, in which I was the first and sole mover in obtaining a new and better encampment in every respect.

One day in the old camp I saw men going and coming from the reservoir, which was on another elevation, drop down with their bucket of water, unable to go further until some one came to their help. There was but one place to obtain water, as far as I could ascertain, and that was the well at the house.

Here comes another patient, but he is not a soldier. This is not a civil hospital, but the man is very sick and must have care. There is plenty of room, and I'll care for him until he can do better. I asked for his name and residence. He was assistant editor of the Hartford *Courant*. I wrote immediately for his wife to come. I was fearful that he would not live. The little woman answered my letter by her presence, and by good care and nursing he was able to return to his duty in a few weeks.

Another wedding is to come off to-morrow evening in the chapel, and another invitation is sent to me. So my lady friend and myself were to witness another ceremony. The clergyman who married the other two couple had gone. But they, at last, found a colored minister who was to perform the ceremony out of an Episcopal prayer book, which was very lengthy. He was unable to read, only as he spelled every word. "Oh my, I can't stand this; we shall be here until sunrise to-morrow!" I looked around for some one to help the poor, embarrassed minister. I caught a glimpse of Captain Doty. I stepped up to him and asked him to go with me to help that man through with that ceremony. "Do, or we shall stay until sunrise. I'll introduce you, and you read the ceremony and let him repeat it after you, and then let him pray and that will end it." "Yes," said he, "but the light is bad." "Well, I'll take a light from the mantel and meet you there; now go." I stepped quickly, got an extra candle and meet the captain in the middle of the floor under the chandelier. I said, "Excuse me, friend, we have come here to help you." This is Captain Doty who will read for you, and you repeat after him, and then make the prayer." "Oh, thank you, Missus!" The ceremony then went off all right and satisfactory to both preacher and people. The next day it was chronicled that it took three persons to marry a darkey couple. The minister, Captain D., and Miss L. This ended the wedding for the present.

At this time I was looking forward to a vacation. In this I had been disappointed. I did not look forward with much assurance, but a faint prospect of which I may avail myself.

CHAPTER IX.

"Ingratitude! how base a thing thou art."

I must here relate another of my hospital inci-dents, which goes to show that the law of kindness does not always work out the best problem.

There were two Confederate patients — prisoners — brought in for me to care for. One was very passive and gentlemanly, the other a profound fire-eater, and very abusive. Here were two distinct characters. The one, patient and penitent, died, I believe, a true Christian.

The death of the one seemed for a little time to check the viciousness of the other, and I began to be hopeful that he was reforming, but this soon wore off, when he fell back into his old self and commenced his slang remarks. It was: "Yank! give me a drink." I paid no attention. "Don't you hear me?" No reply. "Nurse! I'm thirsty." No answer. "Now say, nurse, please give me a drink." "Certainly." "Thank you. Nurse you're d——d cranky, ain't you?"

"Now see here, young man, I'll give you a word of advice. If you call me 'Yank' again, or utter

10

another oath in my presence, I will report you at
head-quarters. You are treated with kindness
which you illy deserve. Should I report you, you
will not fare quite so well."

Here was a case where the utmost kindness had
not the slightest effect, but the wholesome fear of
being reported and the consequent inconvenience
which might follow produced the desired result.
He was somewhat sullen and silent, but his slang
and profanity ceased. Of course he got well, and I
suppose was, in time, exchanged, perhaps a wiser, if
not better man.

CHAPTER X.

"But alas; what holy angel
Brings the Slave this glad evangel?
And what earthquake's arm of might
Breaks his dungeon-gates at night?"—*Longfellow.*

COLORED PEOPLE'S RELIGIOUS MEETING.

It was remarkable how the colored people looked
forward to the day of release. Occasionally I attended their religious meetings at Fairfax Seminary. They were most earnest in prayer for
Massa Linkum.

One would ask the Lord to bless Father Abraham, entreat him to prepare a golden chair in
heaben for Massa Linkum. They were looking so
many years for him and now he had come to set
the people free. Nicodemas must now be woke up
to hear the joyful news. "Call up the dead brud-

der, that he may bless the Lord wid us. The driber's whip will not make our backs bleed no mo. No! No! He may blow de horn for de possum on de gum tree, but not for us. No! No!

"Sisters Sue and Debby what you set so still for? Why you no jump up and say something for de good Lord when He done so much for you? We must not sleep at our posts now for de Debil am a bad boy and if we don't kill him a scare him away he will hab us sure."

Debby gets up, and says, "Some time I'se sorry I'se brack, but when de Lord bless me I'se so happy I forget I'se brack. Den I wonder if we gets to heaben if we be brack thar. I spec we be white, we don't known one anoder thur. But I tinks thar be brack angels thur case Aunt Cassy and Uncle Zed were mity good. I wonder if Massa and Missus will be thur? I tinks if day do day will be awful strang. Day hab better begin to pray here and praise de Lord. Let us neber look back, my brudders and sisters. Oh no! Dare is noting for us to look back to but hardships, toil and de whip, but we keep prayin' till de Lord send Massa Linkum and made us free. I'se so happy, brudders and sisters, dat I feel like jumping up an down."

Up gets sister Sue. "I specs dat de time am close here when we shall see dem dats gone to heaben. Sure poor Dell mus be dar for he keeps prayin' till Massa mos kill him. Does you tink Massa go to heaben? No, nebber, sure; case he be so bad he want to fight. Thar'll be no such tings dar. He go wid his clique where he can smoke, for I tink he'll hab lots of dat sort of folks dar. Only tink how we work hard all de day and hab so little for to eat when Massa lib so high an hab eberyting good, and done no work ony whip us poor bracks. Oh! I wants Massa to hab a good scorchin' sure, den he behaves hisself and lets him done go. I bress de good Lord dat we be free."

" Now will one ob de brudders from Massa Ayers' farm tell how he gets on?

" Well, brudder, I'se bout de same. I'se mos sick wid my long trabbles of a hunerd miles, sides helpin' carryin' chillun all dat way and tink de Rebs close on our heels. An den Uncle Ben done go back to fine de little gal what was lef on de spot where we sleep on de groun a liddle time jus when we trabble seventeen miles. Den we tinks we hear de hosses comin' an we start up mighty spry, and de liddle gal was sleepin' in de bushes. We keep on markin' de trees dat Uncle Ben see de way we trab- ble an' cotch up wid us. Sometime we tink Uncle Ben an' de liddle gal am los sure, or de Rebs cotch em, fo we tinks we trabble slow so dat Uncle Ben com up wid us. But de sun go down. Den de two chillen cryin' fo dare liddle sister sure dat day will nebber see Uncle Ben and liddle Fanny no mo, but we keep lookin' back an' we see suthin' dat hab two heads right in de road dat we tuck, comin' after us. De chillun cry dat suthin' was goin' to eat em up. Den what you tink? It was Uncle Ben an' Fanny.

You should see den. Dare was anoder tune. Singin'
an jumpin,' runnin' to meet Uncle Ben wid Fanny on
his shoulders, which made de animal wid two heads.
Den we pray an' bress de good Lord sure. Sunday
night on rebel groun', long way befo we reach Massa
Linkum's quarters; pears like we nebber get dar.
Long way to Massa's, but we sleep nights, de chillun
tire, de good Lord, He help us. Next day we trabble we come to Massa's. We stop wid de colored
people to rest. Den jus' one night an' one day, de
Rebs wus comin', den we pick up de chillun an'
we trabble. We no mo stop till we come to Massa
Linkum's quarters, mos' dead an' starved. But I
bress de good Lord dat I'se here wid yo' to-night.
We mus' be faithful, cause He done so much for us."

"Now anoder brudder tell us his 'scapes an
blessins."

Uncle Jim speaks. Uncle Jim: "I'se had narrer
'scapes. I'se sure de good Lor' help dis chile, or
I'se nebber been here dis yere night. I'se run from
de farm an' ole Massa in de nite. I tinks I could
cotch de Yanks, den I'se would be safe sure. I
gets a smart way, den I'se hears de houns barkin'.
I gets up in de tree. I pray de good Lor' to help
dis pore nigger. I'se hear de guns all roun' an' de
barkin'. I'se tinks, Jim, you'se done gone sure. I
prays de good Lor' takes dis yere pore brack nigger.
Den jus' I look an' dare comes right up to de tree
lot of boys, blue coats an' guns. Sure Jim, you're
done gone now. Day call out, 'Hello, Possum!
come down, we wants you.' Good Lor! day's goin'

to eat me for possum. I'se comin' down de tree. I
tinks de Lor' no hear dis pore nigger bray dis yere
time. Den I gets down drembling so, I falls down.
Days take me by de han' an' say, ' Pore brack boy !'
Den, no 'fraid, we no hurt you, come wid us, we
take care ob you. I goes wid dem. I tinks an'
wonders who dem be. Day be Rebs day shoot me ;
day mus' be Yanks. Den I tinks, no, day hab no
horns on dare heads. Massa say dat Yanks hab
horns, an' awful critters. I tinks de good Lor' hab
send dem to save dis yere pore nigger. I trabble
wid dem. Days gib me shoes to wear, widdles to
eat till I come yere. Den day say I'se one ob
Father Abraham's chillun. Yes, bredren, I'se berry
happy dis ebenin'. When we gets to heaben an'
sees Massa Linkum an' Massa Jesus, I spec we be
paid for all wese hab to trabble troo here. Dis am
de beginnin' ob de Jubilee. I knows it be comin'
fo long time. De eagle scream it, de wile duck tell
it, eberyting tell *we* be free. We sure dat de Lor'
would come."

" Now, Aunt Zilve, let us hear ob your 'scapes an'
sperances."

" De wonders dat de Lor' do fo us pore bracks.
Well, Massa come one mawning and say to us, he
look bery down an' say, ' Zilve, I spec yore Massa
an' Missus mus' go to Richmon', cause de Yankees
am comin' sure, an' some ob you better go to de
house an' keep it fo us, caze day no hurt you. Us
white day be after cotching. Yo' an' Pete go right
off.' Den we go to de house. Massa an' Missus

take all day can wid dem. Day lef' a mighty heap
behine, lots ob wine an' cider in de cellar, ham an'
poke in de smoke-house, and nice tings in de house.
We tinks de year ob Jubilee be on our heels.
Massa say, 'Take good care ob de house ; you'se hab
good pay when we'se come back.' Yes, bredren an'
sistren, yo' knows what dat pay is. De sweat dat
comes out ob our pore brack skin, an' de driber's
whip, till de brud runs down our heels. Dat am
de pay we gits. I no say dat, but I tink, ole Massa,
you'se hab de long end ob de rope. Now we take
mighty good care ob de way we pull dis rope. We
lib mity high ob de good tings. Den de Linkum
boys cum an' say, 'Done yo' wan' to be free?' Dat
be better dan de wine an' cider, case dat be mos'
gone, an' de key ob de smoke-house Pete tro in de
well. Den we takes close an' widdles an' trabble
night an' day till we gets here. I'se tell yo' bredren an' sistren, de good Lor' helps us pore bracks to
all de tings we hab. He know how Massa an'
Missus 'buse us, an' now we'se gwine to hab our good
tings."

"De darkey get so lonesome liben
    In de log house all alone,
    So day move dare tings in Massa's parlor,
    For to keep dem while he's gone.
    Dares wine an' cider in de cellar,
    An' de darkeys da'll hab sum,
    I specks it all be cornfiscated
    When de Linkum sogers come.
    Ole Massa run, ha — ha,
    De darkeys stay, ho — ho,
    It mus' be now dat de kingdom's comin'
    An' de year ob Jubilo."

"Well dat be good, my sister, but we musen't forget dat de good Lord say we mus' pray fo' dem dat
hurt us. Now will we hear from anoder what de
Lord done for dem?"

"Well, brudder, I tinks sometime what de preacher
said one time, dat ef day strike yo' on one cheek,
den let dem strike yo' on de odder. I'se not ob dat
'pinion. When de Massa strike on de two cheeks
an' den on de back till de blood run down on de flo,
I tinks I no pray him. I wants him to hab sum ob
de same medcin'. We work hard all de day, den
we go home an' bake de hoe-cake, den by de time
we gets our supper an' see to de chillun, den how
much sleep we gits? Massa gets de money, good
dress-up an' good widdles, an' we bracks gets all dat
for Massa, an' he do noting but whip us. I tink it be
time de good Lor' wake up on dis subjec' and send
Massa Linkum to do away wid such persecution.
I tinks de Lor' do right, but I tinks we bracks do
wrong, way back perhaps dats we gets punished.
Maybe I's wrong, but if de debil gibs Massa a
shakin' up all ober I'se satisfied. I tink he gets mo
as dat."

"Well, my good brudder, we mus' do right, ef
Massa do wrong to us, ef we spec' to go to heaben.
Now anoder brudder tell us ob de way ob his trials."

"Brudder Sam tells my 'sperance zackly. Massa
sent me to get de hoss. Den I comes wid de
mule. He so mad dat he say he sell ebery child
I'se hab. I tell Nabby dat the poor chillun Massa
goin' for to sell. She say, 'Tom, let us pray de

good Lawd dat he trow a big stumble-stone in Massa's road. He no safe as he tinks he be. I dream las' nite dat Massa war going up de hill fo' Richmon'. Dat mean sumting, an' I hear de eagle scream dis yere mawnin' so hard dat it shook me all ober. Dat all tells dare be trubble ahead. Ebery-ting 'pears hab tudder color dess yere days. Oh I tinks dat de year ob Jubilee be at de do'.' 'Yes, but de chillun, Nabby, what yo' do fo' dem?'

"'Tom, where yo' tinks he sell dem? Dare be trabblin' to de Richmond. De wa' be on dem 'ready, den de next ting yo' hab to go an' kill de Yankees.'

"'Nabby, you tinks I'se kill dem dat be our friens? Nebber! Ef dare be a chance we hab better try an' go Norf. I tinks Massa want de hoss for to go him journey. Dare Massa comin' now. Where de chillun?'

"'Nebber yo' mind, he no wants dem. Massa look troubbled."

"'Tom, I want you an' Nabby to go an' take care ob de house. Missus an' I be goin' to Rich-mon'. De Yankees ar' comin' but day wont hurt yo'. Here be de keys. Take good care ob de house an' tings. I'se pay yo' well. Good bye.'

"'Tom, yo' cryin'? Yo' big fool. Ef Massa come back all right, he giv' yo' good whippin'. Dat what de pay will be. Now yo' jes' mine dis yere nigger. We take the chillun an' go Norf when de Linkum sogers come. Day takes care ob Massa's house.'

"' I say, Nabby, our time be come. Ef it bees not de year of Jubilee, den it bees suthin' jes' as good.' We goes to de house an' dare we find 'nough to eat. Den we looks all ober de house. Day takes not all de good tings wid dem. We find chicken. an' bacon, an' cider in de cellar. Dat cider was mighty strong. It 'pear to go to de head an' den de feet go crooked ; an de Linkum sogers day come mighty strong. Day look zef day hab no mo'. 'I say, Nabby, may be day take us 'long up Norf. Den what yo' do ?'

"'Oh, I go sure ef day takes de chillun.' We gets ready, an' we takes all we can carry when we starts fo' de Norf, an' here we be dis yere bressed night. Father Abraham's chilluns. De Lor' hab been berry good to us to bring us Norf, my bredren. We hab a hard road to trabble, now we mus' be berry good."

" Now will anodder brudder or sister give us anodder 'sperance ?"

Sister Susie begins by singing :

 ' Let us nebber get weary in servin' de Lor'.
 There's a good time comin'," etc.

" When I tinks how much de Lor' hab done for us pore bracks, an' how we doan get whipped no mo', I jes' wants to jump up an' clap my hans fo' joy. We would nebber be here dis yere ebenin' if He no send Massa Linkum. I'se fogiv ole Massa fo' all de bad he done me, but when Missus keeps tellin' him to whip me mo', till my back was all to pieces, I tink she get sumting in de tudder worl'. I'se not jus' right, an' I prays I may be better. We all need to be better dan we be. We're trabblin' to de tudder worl', an' we mus' press on ef we 'tain de prize."

" Now, dere be time fo' a few mo' to speak an' tell dar 'sperance."

Aunt Chloe now speaks.

" Well, I 'grees wid de mos' ob de bredren and sistren, but I hab good Massa an' Missus mos' ob de time. De bad time was when day takes de chillun away from dare mudders, and sell dem away where we nebber see dem no mo'. Dat be so hard. Dat be dat break dese pore brack hearts. We lub our chillun. We hab so little in dis yere wold to lub 'cept our chillun an' de Lor', I'se be glad dat we be where we can hab our chillun ; dat no Massa can take dem 'cept de Lor'. Dat be right. I'se sure dat we be free. I'se see de sign in de sky one dark night. I see terrible fightin'. I tells Jo dat de Lor' He come sure. Den I hear roarin'. Den de eagle keep screamin'. I'se tinks our reckon-day hab cum. Den I dreams 'bout goin' to de Promise Lan' dat I tink 'bout it all de time. Now I'se so happy sure, keepin' de chillun an' we be free. I bress de Lor'. He make us de people yet ef we be faitful. We mus' not forget dat de good Lor' hear prayer. He help us. We forgets Him too offen."

" Now, den, ef dare be anudder one let him speak."

Aunt Esta : " When I'se was a comin' Norf, I say to Brudder Sol, 'After Massa and Missus gwine

to Richmon', I take some of Missus' dresses, case'
I'se worked for dem.' Sol, he tinks no. I sez, 'Yes,
I'se worked for Missus twenty year an' gets noting
but coarse cloes and widdles. Now I takes my pay.'
Den I takes some of Missus' dresses, shawl, parsol
an' oder tings, cause de lef in mighty hurry. Day
say de Yankees be on dare heels. Now, Sol, I feel
sorry for Massa an' Missus. Day war mighty
cleaver to us bracks. Massa feel berry bad dis yere
mawnin'. He say to Missus: 'Dis yere slavery is
bad bizness. It makes all de trouble.' 'Yes,' say
Missus, 'I wish it would be dun. We hab no trouble
wid our bracks, an' we all be better off ef we nebber
had hab to do wid dis bizness, an' no we mus' do
de bes' we can.' Dat wus so. De Yankees cum
marchin' dat berry night, but day no hurt us bracks.
Day help demselbes wid de widdles, dat be all.
Den day for goin' to take Sol. De I say, 'He my
brudder, an' I am 'lone.' Den day say, 'Where am
de Massa an' Missus?' 'Day dun gone to Richmon'.'
Den day say, 'Yo go Norf, you be safe.' Den day
go. I say to Sol, 'Now we go Norf, we be safe sure.'
Hab we no reason to bress de Lor'?"

"Well, now, we will bring dis meetin' to a close
by de las' exercises. Sister Chloe, take de flo' on
dat side wid de sisters, an' fo' ob each party jine
hans an' dance de roun'."

Now they close by jumping round and singing:

"We chase de debil roun' de stump,
An' ebery jump we hit him a thump,
Glory to Massa Lor'."

At another meeting quite a number would speak
of the kindness of their masters and mistresses.

SONG OF THE NEGRO BOATMAN.

BY J. G. WHITTIER.

Oh, praise and tanks, dear Lor' he come
 To set de people free,
An' Massa tink de day ob doom
 An' we ob Jubilee.
The Lor' dat heap de Red sea wave,
 He jus' as strong as den;
He say de word, we las' night slaves,
 To-day de Lor's free men.

De yam will grow, de cotton blow,
 We'll hab de rice an' corn,
Oh, nebber you fear if nebber you hear
 De driber blow his horn.

Ole Massa on he trabble gone,
 He leab de land behind;
De Lor's bref blow him furder on,
 Like cornshuck in de wind.
We own de hoe, we own de plough,
 We own de hans dat hold.
We sell de pig, we sell de cow,
 But nebber a chile be sold.
       Chorus.

We pray de Lor', He gib us sign,
 Dat some day we be free;
De norf wind tell it to de pine,
 De wild duck to de sea.
We tink it when de church bell ring,
 We dream it in de dream,
De rice-bird mean it when he sing,
 De eagle when he scream.
       Chorus.

We know de promise nebber fail,
An' nebber lie de word,
So, like de 'postles in de jail,
We waited for de Lord.
An' now He open ebery door,
An' trow away de key,
He tink we lub Him so before,
We lub Him better free.
Chorus.

CHAPTER XI.

"That life is long which answers life's best end."

DR. SAMUEL FITCH.

I have often spoken of the house doctor at the Kalarama Hospital as being an earnest Christian gentleman, but I must give my readers a more personal sketch of him, for he so impressed me as being the embodiment of true nobility that I feel like paying tribute to his memory.

Dr. Samuel Fitch was a native of Delaware county in New York State, and possessed all the solid stability of his native hills. He came as a surgeon to our hospital, a very young man at the time, fresh from the medical college, but with skill in his profession, and a conscious sense of duty; a close observer of human nature, as he had been a close student, with a heart full of human sympathy for suffering and a hand ever ready to relieve. Station and color had no preferment with him. The poor black man was to him as much a child of

God's creation as was the president of our nation. A staunch temperance man, no one was ever poisoned or mutilated by his brain being fired or his hand unsteady by strong drink.

On one occasion a poor colored boy, the son of a colored soldier, I think, was brought into the hospital, sick with small-pox. The doctor at once took the case in hand, and, although from the first there was little to be hoped, this good Samaritan physician gave this afflicted boy the best possible care, looking after him more personally lest other nurses might neglect the poor colored waif, remaining at his bedside nearly all the last night, administering both medicine to the sick body and consolation to the out-going soul. I well remember the care-worn look in his face and the tremor in his voice when he told me the poor boy was dead.

With the constant changes ever necessitated by war, I was transferred to another hospital. The young physician stayed there. We met no more on earth, but through mutual friends I have learned of his faithful work after the war, both as physician and Christian, of his noble work in Sabbath schools and in whatever work might improve mankind. He went home to his reward in early life, greatly beloved and mourned by friends and acquaintances, but I fully expect to find him in heaven "among the good and true, when the robe of white is given for the faded coat of blue."

CHAPTER XII.

"The outcasts of earth can risk their lives
To save thee from destruction."

A FAITHFUL SLAVE.

Here is a true statement where the love and faithfulness of a slave to his master's children goes without dispute. Uncle Ben had for many years been a good conscientious slave, the body-servant — as they were called — of Mr. Ayers, a lawyer who had migrated with his family and his mother to Virginia, and although not at all averse to owning and being waited upon by slaves, was nevertheless a staunch Union man.

At, or just before the outbreak of the war, this Mr. Ayers was taken sick and died. Before his death, however, he did an act of justice by giving to all his slaves their freedom, and being quite a wealthy man, he owned a large number.

The wife, always delicate, soon followed her husband, leaving three little girls, the youngest an infant, not many months old.

The sole care of the household depended now entirely upon the aged grandmother and the slaves. They did not forsake the wife in her trouble, and when the Lord called her they still stood faithful to the old grandmother and the little ones.

The Ayers blood was loyal to the flag of the Union, and the Confederates well knew it, and proceeded to confiscate everything which they could

VIANNA AYRES.
AGE AT TIME OF ADOPTION, 12 YEARS.

get hold of. Trouble and privation soon finished up the feeble grandmother.

She felt that death was near, and calling the faithful blacks around her, told them that she had only the Lord and them to leave with the little orphans. "And when I am gone," said she, "take the children and what clothing you can carry and try to reach the Union lines. I feel that God will be with you and that you will succeed. Put your trust in Him and take care of the children. He will bring you through."

The grandmother was buried on Saturday, and that same evening, with some provisions and such other things as they could carry, they joined a party of refugees and started for the Union lines. All night long they pursued their weary journey, carrying the small children, who were too young to walk (and the company contained quite a number of such). Some time next morning, being greatly exhausted, having travelled some seventeen miles, with considerable loading, they halted in a thickly tangled wood for refreshments and a little much-needed rest.

After breakfast they laid down for a few hours of sleep, fearing both the Confederate soldiers and the ravenous wild hogs, by which the woods were infested.

After a while Uncle Ben, who was lying with his ear to the ground, thought he heard the tramp of horses, and immediately fright seized everybody. The sleeping children were snatched from under

11

the brush and undergrowth, and the onward march was resumed on the double-quick.

When they had gone a mile or two and no pursuers were in sight or hearing, the excitement began to abate and then, to their great consternation, they found that little Fanny, the two-year-old baby, had been left behind.

The company were still fearful of being followed by their enemies, and would not consent to turn back; then too, they said, the child had probably been devoured before this time by the wild hogs. The two older sisters were overwhelmed with grief at the loss of their baby-sister, and "their cries," said Uncle Ben, "were more than I could bear. It was as much as any man's life was worth to think of facing one of those wild and vicious hogs, to say nothing of the Rebs, but I could not bear to think of losing the baby much better than the sisters could, so I determined to go back and try to find her. I told the rest to go on, but to mark the trees all along so that if I lived to get back to where we then were, I would be able to follow them. I then went back as fast as my feet could carry me. I knew the place when I came to it, as we had left some of the provisions in our hurry to get away. The provisions were there yet, but where was the child? I could see nothing of her. My heart grew sick, for I throught of her poor little body, perhaps torn to pieces by the hogs. I called softly, Fanny! Fanny!! not daring to call loudly lest I should arouse some vicious animal and share the same fate.

At last I saw the grass and bushes, at some distance, moving slowly. Cautiously I made my way toward the spot, not knowing what I might find there, but on nearing the place I saw moving among the bushes the flaxen locks of the baby. With a great throb of joy I bounded to the spot and caught her in my arms. She was crying softly. I asked her why she did not cry loud, and she said, ' 'Cause I fraid the hogs would hear me.'

"I quickly had the little one astride my neck, her tiny hands clenched in my wooly hair — she knew how to ride that way — and didn't I gallup my best till I overtook the rest of the company, and didn't I keep an eye on that little gal all the rest of the time, till I sot her down inside the Union lines at Fairfax?"

This is faithful old Ben, who had travelled a hundred miles and carried this baby most of the way, spelled only now and then by other kind-hearted darkeys. These poor people came into camp, weary, hungry and foot-sore, having travelled night and day a great part of the time, harassed by the constant fear of being caught by the Rebs.

CHAPTER XIII.

At this time I had my little protegee with a friend in Washington, to stay until I went North.

I called on a friend in Washington and met an old gentleman from Brooklyn, a member of Mr.

Beecher's church. He asked me what I intended to do with that little girl. I said, "It is impossible for me to say at present." "How came she to fall into your hands?" "Well," I answered, "her sister came to me with the child and asked me if I would take the little one, as they had no place to stay, only with the family of colored people from Virginia, and they had all left for the Union lines on foot. The slaves had their freedom given them before the death of the grandmother, and as soon as she was buried, they all started for the Union lines. A few days after this conversation they came to my room with the little girl to see if I would take her as my own." "Well," he said, "she was born in slavery?" "I cannot say, for at this time of excitement in connection with my duties, and in the midst of war, I have no means of ascertaining. Of course I could not go into that part of Virginia now, even if I had time to do so." "Well," he said, "let me have her. I'll give you my gold watch for her." "Oh, my! that would be selling her; no, indeed, never. If I conclude to keep her, I shall have her baptized and educated, and train her for future usefulness. I may leave her North with some good Christian family until the war closes. She is too young to go to school or I would select a good place for her at once. I cannot keep her in a hospital with me, for it is not allowed in military hospitals." "Would you take a letter for me to Mr. Beecher and give it to him in person?" "Certainly, Mr. H. I shall call to see

FANNIE V. C. LAWRENCE AYRES.
AGE AT TIME OF ADOPTION, 3 YEARS.

some friends in Brooklyn, while stopping in New York, and shall be happy to oblige you." About this time I began to think it quite necessary to have a rest. My health began to fail. I asked for a vacation of a month, or more, if necessary. This was granted. I was soon in readiness for a trip North. I reached New York at three in the morning, and rested for a few days, and then started to deliver the message to Mr. Beecher, according to promise. I called on Mr. B. and was pleasantly entertained. Mr. Beecher said the letter I had just presented mentioned something about a little girl, and that I spoke about having her christened. He said that in a few weeks he was to have a number of children presented for baptism, and he would like to have my little girl one of the number. I replied, " I would be glad to have him christen my little girl, but I was going to Albany for a few weeks, and it would be uncertain if I returned in time for the occasion." " Well, be here and it will be all right." He walked with me to show me the church, and then I left New York. I remained with my sister a few days, and started for Albany, where I rested a few weeks. I then returned to New York for the purpose of complying with Mr. Beecher's earnest request, for I had fully made up my mind to have him christen the little girl in preference to any other clergyman. The child had just reached her three years as near as I could ascertain. The Sabbath came, and we reached the church. As soon as the time came for recording the name of the child I was shown into a room for that purpose, and remained until we were ushered into the altar of the church, and were last in the long row of parents with their children. As the children were christened they passed out of the altar. I stood alone with the child when Mr. Beecher asked if he could take the child on the platform; not knowing what was forthcoming, of course, I consented. Mr. B. then presented the curse of slavery, that drew within its deadly coil all that was beautiful, bright and lovely, and that this child would have been its victim had she not been rescued by the present effort that was now being made by our government for the rights and liberty of this oppressed people. Twice his remarks were applauded. At the close of the service Mr. B. asked the audience for a liberal contribution for the education of this child. I waited a suitable time, but received no returns; I called on Mr. B., who directed me to the church treasurer. I called, but that official told me that they had not all paid in their subscription, which I was informed amounted to about $1,200. One gentleman informed me that he gave $100, but not one dollar ever reached me. I was deaconed out of it all. Whoever received the benefit of it the public has a right to judge. When I returned to Washington, I, as usual, found plenty to do. I found that there were two girls who claimed to be sisters of my little girl; but my time was too much occupied to look after them for the present.

The committee, of which I was one, thought our

sanitary department was getting low; that if the war was going to last another year or more, we should be under the necessity of stirring up our friends at the North for more goods of the kind that had helped so many thousand sufferers among our soldiers. While this was in contemplation, I started off for Fairfax to find the two girls. The one that was ten years old was where I had left her; the poor child was glad to see me. Just at this time Gen. E. stepped up to me, and asked, "What are you going to do for those girls?" I said, "Where is the other one? I cannot stay long." The sister answered, "She is over beyond Alexandria on the hill." "Well, I don't think that I could get there and back before the hour that the guard would refuse to let me pass. I'll go, and if I fail to get back, we shall stay in Alexandria." It was quite a smart distance, but on we drove, faster and faster, until we reached the foot of the high hill. "Now, driver, you take the road around and I will climb the hill, and get to the house, and have her ready by the time you reach there." I commenced my upward, almost perpendicular flight, and reached the house in time to have Vianna get her few articles of clothing, ready for a flight back to Fairfax. We were just in time to get across the line, and so got back the same night, feeling that we had made a good trip. "Well, general, do you think I would make a good soldier?" "Yes, indeed, a good lieutenant. I am glad that you are going to take those young girls away from this place.

They would be ruined if they stayed here. They
have seen better days, one can judge from their
appearance. Do you know their ages?" "I should
think 10 and 13. If I should live to see the end of
the war, I should like to have them stay with me;
but now, I can only get good places for them in
Christian families." The gentleman with whom I
had this conversation was a Christian officer from
Columbus, Ohio. The next day I started for
Washington with my charges, and provided a place
for them to stay until I could get ready for the
North. Days passed, and the time came for me to
climb another hill. My family of three children
were all in readiness. A large brigade was to pass
through Washington and all were anxious to see
them pass. I prepared a basket of fruit for my
little girl to give to the little drummer boys as they
were passing by We took our stand in front of
the "White House," near the entrance.

A young man had a stand near us; he asked us
only his regular price, but as soon as the soldiers
asked the price, he charged such enormous rates
that the boys were at a standstill. I at once
noticed the salesman's dishonesty, and said, "Boys,
it is for you; don't you pay for any thing." In a
few moments every particle of fruit, cake, lemonade
and ice water had disappeared. "Oh, lady, for
what did you do that?" "For your dishonesty I
did it. Had you charged them for your fruit the
same that you charged me, I should not have meddled with it, but you, a foreigner, living at your

SARAH ANN AYRES.
AGE AT TIME OF ADOPTION, 10 YEARS.

ease, and our boys fighting to save our government, taking the advantage of them! Why, in justice I should have you taken to jail. Let this be a warning to you."

We left Washington for the North. On reaching Gunpowder river, about one-half of the bridge had been burned. The cars passed over the bridge as far as possible, when they came to a halt, and the passengers were ordered to get out and travel on a pontoon bridge over the other half of the river, to take the cars that were in waiting. My little girl enjoyed this new way of traveling on the pontoon, but the other two were afraid and asked me if this was the way the Yankees built bridges, and if they had to pass over many such. I said, " No, that the pontoon was the result of war; that the enemy had burned the bridge to prevent our soldiers from crossing." " Will the Yankees do the same to the Southerners?" "They all destroy property, the Yankees and Southerners the same; such is the result of war. "Well," spoke Sally, "I have not seen a real Yankee yet ; the people I see look nice." " How did you think they would look?" I asked. "Oh, I was told that they had horns and looked awful, but I reckon you are not a Yankee." "Yes, Sally, I am a Yankee; all the Americans are Yankees. Some day I'll tell you how they came by that name." We reached Sharon Springs, tired, hungry and dusty. The oldest girl remained but a short time, before I found a pleasant home for her in the family of J. A. Ram-

sey, at Seneca Falls. Here she was taught everything useful. Mrs. R. had a governess for her
daughter, and gave Vianna an opportunity to
receive a good common education; not only this,
but looked well after the girl's spiritual interest.
Mrs. Ramsey was a member of the Wesleyan
Methodist church. Vianna was baptized and united
with the church, and was also a member of the
choir. She was blessed with a very fine voice.
More of her history in the near future. Sally
remained at Sharon Springs for a short time, and
then was taken to my brother's, where she remained
until I returned from my New England trip.
I now started, taking my little girl with me. I visited,
in part, five of the States, and went as far east as
Bangor, Maine. On my return home, I reached
Hartford on the 14th of April, when the terrible
news came of President Lincoln's assassination, and
that so soon after the close of the war. Now everything wears a gloomy appearance. We were all so
happy to hear that Richmond was taken, which
would close the war, and save precious lives. But
now, one of the great men of the earth has fallen
and the whole country is in mourning. Who can
comprehend this? Why does the Lord permit it?
We know not now, but we shall know hereafter.
I returned to New York State to look after my
girl, for whom I had not provided a permanent home. I said, " Sally, I think of an acquaintance in Massachusetts who I think would take you
and send you to school. Your chance here is not

what I would like to have it. Would you like to go?" "Yes, if you think best." "Well, then, I'll get you ready at once." So all necessary arrangements were made and off we started for Boston, where we stayed until the next morning. After breakfast we left for Lexington, where the family resided. They were willing to take her and have her taught in the seminary, but all the classes were above elementary, so that there was no class that she could enter. She was taught evenings, and did service through the day, amply paying for her board and schooling, which I did not object to for the present. But I must try and get some one who will give her at least a common education.

I am thoroughly tired in mind and body. Now that the war is over I'll have one good rest. I'll go to Titusville to visit my sister, whom I have not seen since before the war. So off I started with my little girl, and soon reached Titusville, Pa. I found my friends well and had a happy time and a good rest. I shall spend the winter in visiting my relatives and old friends, some of whom I have not met for a number of years. I am sorry to part with the Eastmans, for I have enjoyed my rest and improved in health. My next stopping place will be Norwalk, Ohio, to visit the lady who rendered me so much kindness in one of my hospitals at Washington, while her husband was Congressman. Although I started for Farmington, Illinois, I had many friends on my way westward. I reached Norwalk on Saturday and had a pleasant Sabbath with my friend, and attended the Episcopal church and addressed their Sabbath-school. I left on Monday and stopped at Oberlin to ascertain if there was a possibility of getting my girls in school on reasonable terms, but I failed in this, for the school was already flooded. I proceeded on my journey, stopped over night in Detroit and took an early train for Chicago. There was an accident ahead of us that detained us at Ashtabula for three hours. While we were waiting there, two gentlemen came into the car; every seat was occupied; my little girl was asleep opposite me. I awoke her and placed her in with me, and gave them the seat. My little lady was greatly offended and said those gentlemen disturbed her very much, by taking her bed away. Just then a boy came in crying apples. "Oh, will you get me an apple?" "Yes, wait until he gets here." The gentlemen asked the boy how much he wanted for the apples he had left. "Now he has taken all the apples, too," she said. "Go and give those apples to the little girl," said the gentleman. "Oh, just see here, how many apples I have." "Well, what are you going to do with them?" said I. "Eat them?" "No, not yet." "Oh, shall I thank him?" "Certainly." "Then can I eat them?" "No, you cannot." "Shall I tell him I am sorry I was so cross because I had to give up my seat?" "Yes, and ask them to take some of the apples he so kindly gave you." This settled the trouble with her. She became very much interested in her new acquaintance, and asked him if he had a little girl at home. He told her no, but he had a little boy. When we reached Chicago we were two hours late for the train I had intended to take. This gentleman introduced himself as Mr. Whiting, of Chicago. As I was a stranger in the city, and would like to take an early train, he said he would be happy to entertain us at his house until time for the train. My wife, he said, will join me in an acquaintance. The walk from the street cars is just across the park. This was preferable to going to a hotel. I accepted the offer. After quite a long ride in the street cars, we reached the house and met a beautiful lady at the door, who made us very welcome. Being very weary from my long journey, I retired for a little rest, after which I felt quite refreshed, and ready to enjoy a beautiful dinner, which was served at two o'clock.

The little boy, of ten years, and Virga, were not long in becoming acquainted. The lady was a Cuban by birth. Mr. Whiting married her when he was sent to Cuba by the government. She was an accomplished lady. I was well pleased with my new acquaintances; I usually find agreeable company when traveling. One can select very soon, by close observation, the class you wish. We had a fine rest, and left the next morning for Farmington. Mr. Whiting accompanied us to the depot. We left on the eight o'clock A. M. train and reached Farmington at eleven o'clock P. M. At nearly midnight we reached the home of my dear old friends, and rang the bell. The answer came slow. "Who can it be at this late hour? Ask before you open the door — it may be that some one is sick. Who is there?" "A friend." "Who?" "Lawrence, don't give up the ship." "Well, then, you will give yourself up." We were almost pulled into a warm room, and after a warm greeting and a quick, short visit, we retired for the rest of the night.

I am sure I shall return to the old Empire State renewed, for here I am, regaining my health and strength far beyond my expectations. This is too good to last. Virga has a fine voice for a little girl, and sings beautifully, and I'll finish her in the rudiments of music, with her other lessons. The Sabbath came, and all must go to church, which was near by. After service was the Sabbath-school. Mr. B. proposed to have Virga sing one of her Sabbath school hymns, which she did. After the school closed the minister wanted her to sing again. She sang a few more. He then asked her who taught her to sing. She said her mother, "Well, if your mother can teach you to sing like that, she can teach our daughters to sing." It seems quite evident that there will be another hill to climb in this prairie country. One call after another seems to come to me unsought. They said, "We will get up a large class for you if you will teach one term. The chapel of the Congregational church is at your service. It has two large blackboards, and can be well warmed. "Yes, I'll try it." Teach singing school! That is a new business for me. I wonder what next; I ran away from teaching, but it faces me, go where I may. The number of scholars on the list was fifty-two. The notice was given and a singing class was opened. It was a day singing school of girls and boys, ranging in age from 6 to 18. I classed them according to age and commenced my work, and was more successful than I anticipated at the opening. Before we finished the term a concert was spoken of by the scholars, and as soon as the school closed every thing pointed in the direction of a concert. Sacred pieces were selected and practised, also the most popular war songs were in readiness. A queen of May was selected for the occasion. Every one was engaged to do something to make it a success, which, indeed, it proved to be. Twenty-five of the small boys and girls performed the "Rally Around the Flag." Each one had a small banner. They marched around the desk, the platform was large enough to give them plenty of room. This performance was very beautiful, with corresponding costume. I had two classes out of the city, one five miles out, in a country school-house, and one two miles out, in an opposite direction. I was urged to have the second class of young people in the city, but this was to be an evening class, to which I objected.

I have just received a letter from my friend, Mrs. Worcester, of Norwalk, to make her a visit on my return to New York. Soon I shall leave my dear old eastern friends in Farmington forever — Mr. and Mrs. Budd. I have known them from childhood; they were close friends in my father's family. Also one of my early scholars, the Deyos, one family living five miles out of the city, where I had a pleasant visit. There was an incident occurred while I was staying at their house, which I must relate. Mr. Deyo wanted me and my little girl to stay with his wife and the two young girls while he went to Schoharie to visit his aged mother. About this time there was an excitement in that vicinity about the "Kentucky Demon," who was supposed to come in a hideous form. He was also called the Kentucky gentleman. The three little girls had retired and we were alone in the parlor. After a while Mrs. Deyo went through the kitchen into the pantry. She came back frightened almost into a fainting fit. "Oh, Miss Lawrence, the Kentucky demon stood by the pantry window, what shall I do?" "Don't be frightened," I said; "I'll go and see him too. Are your outside doors locked?" "I don't know." "I'll go and see." I fastened the door and then went into the pantry, but found no traces of the Kentucky gentleman. I said to her, "Don't you think that it may have been your reflection in the glass, the night is so very dark?" "Oh, I was so frightened, I cannot say; I surely saw the image of a human being at the window." "Well, he is locked out, and if he comes in he will have to come through the keyhole, and if he does, I'll put him out; now let us give up the search. I am more afraid of the gray wolves that are howling around here at night; I am afraid to go out at night."

The time is nearing for me to start toward home, but one more visit is in anticipation. Mrs. B.'s adopted daughter, living in Bloomington, will wonder why I don't come to see her, now that I am so near. I think she will hardly know me; she was quite a little girl when she left New York. I'll make that my last visit in Illinois. Mr. Deyo returned from the east and I went to prepare for my homeward journey. I went to Galesburg, after bidding adieu to my friends in Farmington, and spent the night at Rev. E. Beecher's and left the next morning for Bloomington. I spent a pleasant week in this town, at Mr. Rood's. When I left Mr. Deyo's at Farmington, he prepared a basket and three little chickens in it for little Virga to take home. To travel a thousand miles, with the care of three extra pets, was quite a charge for me. But one died at Bloomington, notwithstanding they were put out through the day and well cared for. Mr. and Mrs. Rood accompanied me to the cars, and as we came near, we heard singing. Mr. R. asked me which car I wished. The singing car of course. I bade my friends good-bye and entered the car, which had few passengers. We had been seated but a few moments, when a gentleman stepped up to me to shake hands, and said, "You don't know me, do you?" "No, sir." "At a Sabbath-school convention at B.?" "Oh, yes, I do remember, now." "Did you know the Evangelist Hammons, who is pretty well represented in this State?" "I heard of him when he held a series of

12

meetings at Peoria." "He is in this car with his bride on his way to Rockport city. Would you like an introduction?" "Yes." After the usual ceremony, I was asked if I were on my way to the Sabbath-school convention at Rockport city. I said, "No, I am on my way to New York." "Would you like to attend the convention, also Mr. K.'s meeting?" "Yes, but that will detain me a week longer. How far from Chicago is it to Rockford city?" "About eighty miles. If you would like to go, you may go as a delegate, at half fare." "Well, I am in good company." I accepted the offer. I changed cars at Chicago, and had my baggage rechecked for Rockford city, sure of an all-night's ride with a little girl and two chickens to care for. We reached the place just before·daylight, went to the hotel and gave the chicks in care of the landlord, with orders to call me at seven o'clock for breakfast. At nine o'clock we were called upon to go to the church to receive my stopping place during the convention. Then I returned to the hotel for my young family, and was conveyed to Mr. V.'s. I rang the bell, and was very pleasantly welcomed. But the lady said, "I was to have four guests; I wonder if they will come" "Oh, yes, Mrs. V., they are here." "Where?" "In that basket." Which was opened and out came the little prisoners, happy to enjoy their freedom once more. Grandma took charge of them and put them into their beautiful yard of evergreens and strawberry vines. The convention was very interesting, but Mr. Hammons' meeting much more entertaining, and many were brought to know the preciousness of a new life, not children only, but adults. And here I found an old friend, Mrs. W., the daughter of the minister who was my first spiritual teacher.

This was a very unexpected meeting and a pleasant one. It occurred just on the eve of my leaving Rockford city. Next morning I left for the East; only one more stopping-place; I am homesick to see the mountains of my native State. I am not long in getting back to Norwalk, Ohio, with my little family of a little girl and two chickens. This will be a resting place for one week, then I must return home to find a place, if possible, where I can have the other two girls attend school together and have them with me. They have been separated the most of the time since they left Washington. I consulted Mrs. Worcester concerning this matter; I gave her a correct description of the girl as being very handsome and intelligent. She concluded to take her as her own and educate her. Oh, what a relief this was to me! Here she was to have a lovely home where she would not be exposed to evil influences. Her present home was not such as I had hoped for; her education was neglected and her servitude was beyond her years. This removed a burden from me. One good home for the poor lonely orphans. Vianna, the other girl, is doing well for the present. I remained in this noble family over a week. In the meantime a fine entertainment was given for me. Virga's chickens were given for a remembrance to the judge, and he, in return, made her a fine present. This family were formerly from Massachusetts, and expected to return in the near future. I left with brighter prospects for the present, but how little we know of the future. I had a friend to consult in whom I had confidence, and was feeling better able to battle with coming events.

CHAPTER XIV.

I was on my way to Adams, Jefferson county. A gentleman asked me if I was on my way to conference. I said, " No, sir ; I am on my way to Adams." " Conference is in session at that place," he replied. Then I said, " Do you expect a new appointment?" " No," he said, " my appointment is more permanent ; I have charge of Falley Seminary." " I had heard quite often of the school, and I should· be glad to see it if I had time ; I may send a pupil ; at present my time is fully occupied," " Well," he said, " give me a call before you go elsewhere."

We are at our stopping-place. Mr. and Mrs. Burchard I found well and glad to meet me. Mrs. B. was very much interested in the little girl's singing. Here I had an urgent invitation to give a lecture on the war. Conference held its sessions most of the time in the Presbyterian church, it being larger than the Methodist Episcopal church, but both churches were used during conference. Mr. B. had his pupil ready for her part, and the ap-

pointment was made for meeting in the Presbyterian
church at two P. M. Conference adjourned for the
occasion. The house was filled, every inch of it.
I had never before addressed such a body of gentle-
manly-looking clergymen. While Mr. Burchard was
speaking and the little girl of five years old, standing on the table singing, I took a view of the large
audience before me ; I thought, Miss L., you have
a steep hill to climb this time, but Lawrence must
not give up the ship now. My time came, I was at
home with my friends, I had nothing to fear. I was
engaged in a good cause, and the Lord will always
help us when we are helping those who need our
help. We can always find some one to encourage
us by word or deed. If we are laboring for the
good of some poor soul and the glory of God, we
shall have our reward. I remained with my friends
during conference, and, with them, was invited to
dine with the bishop and his staff at Mrs. S.'s ; and
also with the same party at Mr. Burchard's. There
was a very friendly feeling between the different
churches, for which, I think, Adams is noted. I feel
an attachment for Jefferson county. It was there
where I first commenced my public temperance
labors, and I often think of this people as zealous
workers in the reforms of the day. At this time of
my short stay at Adams, I was invited to give another lecture at Watertown. Mr. B. accompanied
me; my little girl sang a number of war songs.
She had a remarkably strong, yet sweet voice, and
performed her part finely. An engagement was

made by one of the clergymen at the conference for me to speak at Potsdam, but the inclemency of the season prevented me from going.

At this time I began to feel weary. When I take a view of the past, from my childhood up to the present, my life has been one continual scene of excitement. There was one character pointed out by the Saviour that I always tried to shun. That was the hypocrite. The amount of iniquity practiced under an assumed name, I abhor. I have frequently been told that I was too much outspoken and made enemies. This was often said at the time I worked in the temperance reform. I am apt to call things by their right names. With a certain class this will not be well received. I have no wish to become popular through deceit. I once gave a lecture, that was cutting, on immorality, at which a young man took offense and said more than the law would allow him. I was urged to take the matter in hand, but I chose my own way of doing it, which I'll have inserted, if I have not lost the poem.

On my way back to Seneca Falls, I called at Falley Seminary. The professor made me a liberal offer, if I saw fit to have one or more of the children enter at any time I was ready to accept, but about this time, I received a letter from Mrs. W. of Ohio, stating that a friend of hers had been to Lexington after Sallie, but the doctor and his wife would not let her go, saying that she belonged to them. There was no papers of any kind whereby they could hold the child, but I should not have thought of removing her, if they had done according to agreement. I had no objection to her making herself useful, but I objected to having her in continual servitude, and thereby neglecting almost wholly her education. For this reason I would have her removed to where she would be cared for and treated as a member of the family. I wanted Vianna and Sallie to attend school together, and had already made preparation for this at Falley Seminary. Vianna was already at school, and the little one was too young to go to school, but was taught at home. Vianna was improving finely and would have finished her education here, but for the interference of outsiders. There was a school teacher who had an insane brother who could not be left alone and needed close attention. This teacher and another woman had taken advantage of my absence and almost persuaded the young girl to take a position so dangerous and improper. On my return, Vianna informed me of the new project. " Well, do you want to go ? " . " No, I don't want to go and take care of a crazy man. I am afraid of crazy people." " On what terms will she take you ? " I asked. "She will hear my lessons evenings, and I am to help do her work." Just then came two ladies for a call; the wife of the principal being one ; they made a short call. Vianna says, " Miss Lawrence, those are the two ladies that wanted me to take care of that one lady's brother." " Why did they not ask me about your going ? " " They came to get me to go, I think, not knowing that you were here." "Well, would you have gone in my absence?" "No, indeed; I said when they were here before, that you would not consent to my going." "Well, Vianna, I think we shall leave here, if this is the way matters are working. I am not willing to have you go to school here any longer. The movement of these two callers is thoroughly crazy, one that would endanger your life, and perhaps, what would be worse, your morals. I'll have you go back to Mrs. Ramsey's for the present. I have a mind to buy a place at M. where I have just been, and after I get settled and rested, I'll see that you have another chance at school, but under the present circumstances you cannot stay here. The idea of having a young girl take care of a crazy man and drudge all day, and they only hear your lesson in the evening! I call that slavery in the first degree. Now, you pack your trunk and get ready to go." She went to Seneca Falls, and I and my little girl to Mexico, where I purchased a cottage and an acre of ground, which was well supplied with fruit. Here we had plenty to do. It was early spring, quite a little time before I could make improvements or make a garden, but the time came at last, and work commenced, the ground was made ready for planting, and a clergyman living in the country near by supplied me with garden seeds. But I do not know how to make a garden. I'll watch and see my neighbors work; but my near neighbors had already made theirs. Just then came a heavy rain followed by a cold spell. I think my garden will have to stay over until another year. But soon prospects began to brighten; the weather began to get warm and there was every indication of a prosperous fruitful season, but too late for my garden, I thought.

One day my next door neighbor came in, saying, " Miss Lawrence, I have brought you a present; come and see." On going to the front door I saw a carriage. I expected a package. I stepped to the carriage, and, behold! a living package met me. My sister! a joyful meeting. She came to spend the summer. Now I shall have some one to show me about the garden. My neighbor said that the people who occupied the place before me never had a garden. " Well, I'll try it ; my sister understands the business, and we'll have one." I had the ground prepared ; this was the first of June. Those that had their gardens made before the cold rain were almost a total loss, and mine, that was delayed for want of knowledge to do the work, paid well for being late. Every thing that was put into the ground yielded plentifully; flowers bloomed in the front yard. This was a pleasant home. A letter comes from Lexington, Mass., stating that Sallie was sick and wanted to come with me for the summer; the doctor thought the sea breeze in-jurious for her, as her lungs were in a bad condi-tion. Certainly she can come. The doctor's wife came part way with her and then left her to go to Mr. Ramsey's to meet her sister, who was staying there. She stayed with her a few weeks before she was able to come to Mexico. She was well cared for by Mrs. R., and hopes were entertained for her final recovery when she and her sister started for my house. They arrived in safety, but very much fatigued. The family were together once more. Vianna and Sallie had not met each other since they came North four years ago. They had a pleasant time while they were together. Vianna enjoyed her visit and returned to Seneca Falls. Sallie remained until late in the fall. She said to me, " I would like to go back to Lexington ; that is my home." " Why, Sallie, why not stay here ? " " Well, I would rather go back." I saw that her mind was fully made up to go back. I made preparations to take her back, and in a few days we started ; we reached Albany before dark, stopped at my brother's until ten o'clock, then took the palace car for Boston. She rested well during the night, and directly after breakfast we took the train for Lexington, reaching there before noon. The seminary had, a short time previous, been burned. Of this I was not aware until I reached the place. The school was removed to another locality. I remained until the second day. As I was making preparations to leave, the doctor asked me to take a walk. I said, " Yes ; a short one, for I must start for home to-day." We had gone but a short distance when he said, " You must take Sallie back with you." " Take her back ; for what ? " " Well, she is consumptive and we can't have her die here."

"You contemptible villain; how dare you speak like that about the poor child. Don't I know how you refused to let Mrs. Worcester have her. There she would have been treated as their own daughter and educated. You told the person who came after her that she belonged to you. Did you not promise me that she should be taught at the seminary, but instead of that, you had her stand behind your chair, to come and go at your bidding, and to-day she can hardly read or write. I'll give you to understand that I did not bring those children from the South to be slaves at the North. They are orphans but not friendless and are children of good ancestors. If they had a drop of African blood, their honest and upright principles would cast such as you into total darkness; besides you have those in your family, who, had they been South before the war would have been put upon the auction block. As long as Sallie was able to do your bidding, you were ready to keep her. As soon as her health fails, you cast her off, and that, after she was offered one of the best homes that could possibly be had." This debate occurred during our walk, which came to an end very shortly. Thus ended my first controversy with Dr. Lewis, of Lexington fame. I went to Boston to ascertain if there was any hope in the case of the young girl. My little girl was with me, and from the previous excitement, the child began to cry. The doctor saw her and said to her, "What is the matter, little girl? Come here to me." "Tell me, can you help my sister?" "Certainly," he said, "if it is in my power, with God's blessing." Then he inquired into all her symptoms, age, etc. He said her case was doubtful, but he would take her and do all in his power, if Dr. Lewis would sign a paper that the girl was incurable. My pent-up feelings gave way. I wept like a child, and finally we all three were weeping. I returned to Lexington, and gave the paper to Dr. Lewis, who refused to sign it, consequently the little girl's doom was sealed. I left for home and in a few weeks I had a letter from Mrs. Ramsey, that Vianna had been sent for to come immediately, for her sister was in a dying condition, and Vianna was already there. In a short time another message came that Sallie was dead and buried, and she, Mrs. Ramsey, should look for Vianna's return home very soon. She did not come, but, instead, came a long letter from Dr. Lewis, that he thought of adopting Vianna. He would give her a finished education and she should associate with the best in the land, and should travel with him and have all the accomplishments that were necessary.

Mrs. Ramsey thought this a good opportunity for Vianna, and said that she would not stand in the way of her improvement. But I asked, "Why did not Sallie have just a small share of all that?" Poor child that she was, she had to trudge through the deep snow in winter to a public school, and it was in this way that she took cold, which was one of the causes of her death. She was neglected and has gone to a premature grave. I say again, why was not she adopted and given all those advantages? She was just as beautiful, and more so, than Vianna. We will keep an eye out and see if there is not a selfish motive in all this. Why all the fair promises were not fulfilled in the case of the beautiful, loving and obedient Sallie, will be answered at the day of judgment. I am glad there will be a day when all things shall be made right. It is a happy thought, that the poor departed child is adopted, not by mortals, but by her heavenly Father, who has given her a home far above that which earth can give. The eldest and youngest are to struggle for life, and what will be their lot is yet to be realized. It is a blessing that we do not know what is in store for us in the future. It comes too soon and often finds us unprepared to meet it. We need the presence and aid of our divine Saviour every moment.

But a short time, perhaps a year, after this I called at Mrs. Ramsey's and to my happy surprise I met Dr. Lewis' adopted daughter. I was delighted to see her. She was apparently happy and very well-dressed. I asked her, " How long since you left Lexington?" "Oh, I am not there now; I am staying with Grandma Lewis." I replied, "I know Mrs. Lewis. Did you attend school at Lexington?" "No; only a short time; they had me come to Auburn to stay with the old lady." "How much of a family is there?" "Oh, the family is small; the old lady's niece is there and goes to school." "What is your work?" "I do housework and sewing and whatever is necessary." "And what is your wages?" "Nothing." "And how is it that they call you Mary Lewis?" "I write my name Mary Ayers Lewis." "Did the doctor have your name changed lawfully; that is, did he take papers and have it rightly confirmed according to law?" "Oh, no; nothing like that." "Well, Vianna, unless they send you to school and treat you as a daughter I shall take the matter in hand. You are not entitled, by law, to one cent of his property. He is a fraud, and has failed in every point, in fulfilling the promises in his letter, of which I have a copy. He held Sallie as a servant, and that without pay, and has taken you under false pretense. Instead of taking you as a daughter, to be educated, and travel and be introduced into the best society, he has taken you as a slave; he sends you to take care of his aged mother, to relieve him of the burden. Now, Vianna, if you do not attend school at once — no putting off — I'll raise a breeze that will equal a cyclone. You are now almost or quite eighteen years old, and if you ever expect to have an education it is time to attend to it." Soon after this I heard that Vianna was attending school and getting along nicely.

A year or more passed and all went on as usual. I rented my place in Mexico and located in Seneca Falls. This was the first year that my little girl went to school. I had taught her at home. She entered the department next to the highest in the academy and made fine. progress. In January we received word that Vianna was very sick and her recovery doubtful. We hastened at once to Auburn to see her. She had a bad cough and every indication of a speedy death. All remedies seemed useless, as there were no changes for the better. Her food did not seem to benefit her. After a time her cough abated somewhat, and then a change for the better gave us hopes of her ultimate recovery. The weeks came and went with but little change for the better. But it came at last. The month of March, that terrible one of the whole year, will give her a trying time. But she passed through, gaining slowly. I had charge of her for three months, and although a sacrifice to me, I had the pleasure of seeing her on the way to recovery. I met her distinguished adopted father before I left, and there were two icebergs met without sufficient sunshine to melt them. Lawrence knew that she was right and would not "give up the ship." If I had not looked after the interests of those orphan children they would have had a hard time; they passed through hardships at the best.

Vianna's recovery was of short duration; she caught a new cold in May and it never left her. She lingered until September and left this world of trials for a better inheritance. As long as she was living at Mrs. Ramsey's she enjoyed excellent health. Southern-born children, not being accustomed to our climate, need constant watching until they become acclimated. I always watched my little girl, and the first appearance of a cold was never neglected. I have not to regret that I ever neglected her.

Trials, sickness and death will come notwithstanding all that we can do, and all that we love on earth will soon pass away. My little girl felt very bad when the last sister was gone. Mr. Ramsey's carriage, with two members of his family, myself and little girl attended the funeral. The "Good Templars," of which Vianna was an official, attended in a body. The services were impressive. We returned home with sad hearts. I was fearful that the next in the near future would be the little one, but her health was good and with good care I may be happily disappointed. How many mourn the loss of children, when it may be the greatest mercy that they have gone so early.

I feel a strong attachment for my poor little lone one. But this she probably does not realize now, as she will be likely to in coming years, should she live. I do not wish the two sisters back again. They are free from toil and care; they are where the wicked cease from troubling and the weary are as rest; they were of French and Yankee blood. The Bible says that all nations were made of one blood, and it furthermore says there will be gathered together all nations, kindreds, tongues and people. There will be no distinction. The Saviour when on earth chose the poor. You will see many Mary Magdalens and some, and I doubt not many, very many black angels in the kingdom, and you yourselves thrust out, and the black angel may be the first one that you will call on to bring a drop of water to cool your parched tongue. No doubt there will be many a Lazarus in heaven, and many despisers of the Lord Jesus will take their place with Dives. If those who profess Godliness would take the Bible for their guide, there would not be so much ignorance concerning those matters. A lady who had been a professor of religion for a long time said to me one day, " Miss L., how is it that the Bible doesn't speak of praying?" "Of praying?" said I, with astonishment. "Yes," she said, "I never read any. thing about praying." "Then you never read your Bible. I'll tell you the one great trouble with you, is the reading of those miserable yellow-covered novels, and all novels are messengers of evil; it takes all your leisure time to read them. They are the gods you worship, and they will lead you to temporal and eternal ruin." "Oh, now, you are too bad," she said. "What! too bad when I tell you the truth. I am doing my duty. Now read your Bible, *that* will tell you that you cannot serve God and Mammon." "Why, do you think I'll be lost?" "I do, unless you repent and be converted, as the Bible teaches." How the matter ended with her I cannot say, but this is not a solitary case; too many have more novels than Bibles.

Some have a very expensive Bible in their parlors for an ornament, but never read it, as if that would be their salvation. I have been pleasantly informed

13

by many of my friends that I was too outspoken, but I believe in calling things by their right names. I do not believe in putting a silver covering over spoiled meat. But I have charity for the helpless ones. Too often a poor person takes an improper step; and those who have to struggle through unseen trials are censured by those who know nothing of the hardships of life. There is a case that I am too well acquainted with to be mistaken. It was this: A young woman had an abandoned husband; he eloped with another man's wife; of course, the lawful wife had no trouble in getting a bill. A gentleman says to me, "Do you know that there are unfavorable reports about her character?" "I do not; can you tell me what they are?" "No; I cannot." "Well, sir, there were bad reports about your wife before you married her; can you tell me what they were, and do you believe them?" No answer.

The Saviour, when called upon to judge a woman for a serious crime, said to her accusers, "Let him that is without sin cast the first stone." How true it is that many people are ready to accuse others, when they themselves are guilty of the same sin. The time is not far distant when the final account will come, and be sure that the Judge of all the earth will do right. If many of the accusers of the present day were called upon to cast the first stone, there would be a stir to seek a hiding-place. They forget that there is a recording angel taking note of unrepented sins. Read your Bible; the

New Testament is all that is necessary to teach us
our duty and regulate our lives.

Thus far I have given the sunny part of my life.
I have passed over much that might interest some
of my friends of the present day, but the friends of
my youth and middle age have mostly passed away.
My father's family have all gone long ago. My
army hospital life has left its mark upon me. I receive a small remuneration, for which I am thank-
ful, but not sufficient for the demands of my ad-
vancing years.

The little one that I adopted and educated, married one whom I opposed, knowing his reckless life
rendered him wholly unfit for one like her. When
sick and among strangers he deserted her and an
infant daughter and eloped with a woman, who left
her husband and two small children. My three little Southern children are all laid away, for which I
thank my heavenly Father. They have just gone
before me; I know now where they are, and soon I
shall meet them beyond the reach of their perse-
cutors. The one poor child, the double orphan, is
left to grapple with the world, unprotected and un-
provided for, only as far as the small savings of her
mother's hard labor will go. May God sustain the
poor child, left at an age when a mother's care is
most needed. Oh, ye daughters of wealth and
pleasure, does not this speak to you to open your
hearts and hands, to work in the capacity of the
good Samaritan, and with faith and charity, dispense of your abundance among the worthy chil-

dren of misfortune, and when the Lord shall come
to judge the world, He will say, " Forasmuch as ye
have done it unto the least of these, ye have done
it unto Me, enter into the joy of your Lord."

Now comes my life among the aged. There were
to be eleven vacancies by death, before I could
enter.

About this time the newspapers were advertising
that all the first nurses of the late war were to receive a pension of $25 and $20 a month ; that is,
those who served from one to two years. I was
one of the first and served all through the war. I
wrote to Washington. The answer came that I
should do all that I could, and that Mrs. C. would
work for me there. I wrote to her that my papers
were on file at the capital and I wished her to go
there and get them. I heard no more about my
pension at that time. In a short time I received a
letter asking me to return to Albany (I had gone
for a few weeks to a neighboring town) at once, as
there was a room in readiness for me at the
" Home." Well, I thought there must have been
an epidemic to take so many in so short a time. I
had supposed that it would be at least two years
before eleven would die. I had a mind not to answer the call, but I came and was accompanied to
the " Home." The room was shown me, but it
had an unhealthy air. I asked if the walls had been
whitewashed. They said no — the room had been
shut up, which gave it an unpleasant air.

A few days after this, I entered my new home,

and in a short time I became restless, nights; something unusual for me. On close examination, I
found some small insects that I did **not** care to
have for company. By perseverance I soon got rid
of them. Another thing, I was not permitted to
have a light in my room, had gas-lights in the hall,
where **we** could sit, but had to take the draught;
I tried it and took a very bad cold; another attempt
ended in sickness. There was plenty of food provided, but it was badly prepared. At one time I
noticed on the kitchen table lay a pile of nice quarters of lamb. Now, I thought, we shall have a good
dinner. But, alas! it came on the table hard and
dry. The potatoes, as usual, came dressed in their
skins, which made it difficult to tell the good from
the bad. It is a fact that a large share of the
potatoes that came on the table were not fit to eat.
I could stand this no longer. I said to the matron
that it was not safe to eat those potatoes; that by
cutting the ends she could tell the good from the
bad; that it would certainly create an epidemic.
This was done for a short time, then the old practice was resumed. The bread had a peculiar taste.
The coffee did very well. The tea I seldom drank.
However, I fared very well. I had friends who
supplied my wants, and more than I could possibly
use myself. My cousin, Mrs. Peter Sandhovel,
from Mexico, Oswego county, sent me a basket
that I could scarcely carry to my room, filled with
good things of the earth. Miss Amelia Cook was
another who came semi-monthly to supply my

wants; and others, too numerous to mention, remembered me kindly. I did not forget the poor
friends around me, who were less fortunate. I
would sometimes, and, indeed, quite often, step
across the hall and make a couple of beds; one was
occupied by Miss Brown and the other by Miss
Lansing. In making the bed of Miss B.'s I found
a number of bugs; the next time that I made it I
found them more numerous. I said, "Mandy, do
you sleep well nights?" "Yes, pretty well." I
made another search; took up a large under pillow,
with a casing, and beheld a regiment. Oh, my!
how could you sleep? I opened the window and
cast it into the back yard, and called the matron.
She said to me, " Did you cast that pillow into the
yard?" "I did, for your inspection; and in that
dish there is a regiment of over thirty having a
fine swim." " Well," she said, " Miss Lansing has
brought them into the house." Said I, "That can't
be possible, for she has been here but a few days;
and those in the swim are old customers, from
great-grandfathers down to the fourth generation."
Miss Lawrence exit. I went to my room. Here
is another hill to climb, but " Lawrence won't give
up the ship." The dear old lady next door to Miss
B.'s says to me, " Miss Lawrence, I cannot sleep;
there is something disturbs me." " Speak to the
matron," I said. " I am afraid to." I said, " Speak
to her; she will see what is the matter with you."
Miss Lansing was assigned to the third floor, a persecuted person. There was trouble again; her bed

was hard and untidy, and the same trouble that afflicted Miss B. and her neighbor. I could stand it no longer. I said to her, " Miss Lansing, you have influential friends living in Albany; I shall call upon them and have them see that you have better treatment." I set out and saw a lady who responded at once, and Miss Lansing had better accommodations, but still had enough to contend with until her death.

There was a funeral at the " Home." The inmates, as usual, took their seats in the corridor. There were a few of us who always occupied the sofa near the parlor door. At this time there was room for one or two more. I happened to see Miss Lansing sitting in the draught, and knowing that she had a bad cough, I stepped up and invited her to take a seat with me out of the draught, which she did gladly. After service, and the people had left, the matron asked me if I had invited Miss L. to a seat on the sofa? I said, "Certainly." "Well," she said, "don't you do that again." " Yes, I shall," said I. Another time, after Sabbath service, the clergyman asked what intelligent looking lady that was, who came in late and was seated on the front seat. The matron began with her slang. The gentleman turned away and heard but little of it. I expected my turn would come next for interfering, but my time had not yet come.

I was asked to watch with a sick inmate. I said I was not feeling very well, and if they could possibly do without me, I wish they would, and I would watch the next night. The next evening I offered my services and was rejected. I was taken quite sick with a heavy cold and had my own physician, to which I had a right. He said my lungs were in a bad condition, and I was liable to have pneumonia, but being a nurse myself, I knew how to avoid danger. I was neglected, but I had all I wished for the present. I always had a supply on hand and was able to care for myself, but knew that I must not go into the basement. At this time the matron came with the hired man and had the gas fixture put in a condition not to be used. But I gave myself no trouble. The next day she took my doctor down into the basement to get his consent to have me come down to meals. In this she was disappointed. The next move, a few days after, she came into my room with Dr. W., who made occasional visits to the "Home." She took a bottle of essence that was on the stand, and seeing that it was not my medicine, she said, " Get that medicine for your face, the doctor said it was not necessary." I was at this time convalescent, and not taking medicine, and the doctor was too much of a gentleman to interfere.

" Now, Miss Lawrence, let the doctor have your pension papers to get your pension." I replied, " My pension papers are in Washington, and I shall go there myself before long, and do all that is necessary." I soon after began to get ready to go to Washington. A call from the matron, " Miss Lawrence, how long do you expect to be gone to

Washington?" "I cannot say." "Well, if you stay more than four weeks you lose your room." "How is that?" I asked; "Miss B. was gone six weeks, came back for a few days, and is gone for a longer time — but I don't mind about the room, that is all right." Soon after this, two of the committee came to my room, and one of them said, "Oh, dear, Miss Lawrence, I have something to say to you, and I am afraid you won't like it; you are to give up your room and take one on the third floor." "Oh, and is that all; that is not bad," said I. A few weeks before this, I was sent down into the basement to wash dishes, with my next-door neighbor. She was feeling very bad, and it having been made up between the two, the matron was present. My neighbor was seated by the table wiping cup plates; she commenced crying, her hands hurt so bad. "Well, go up stairs; you need not wipe dishes," said the matron. The inmates were afraid to complain for fear they would lose their place; they had nowhere to go. There was a mixed multitude to care for, and it required a most judicious person to administer to their wants. It represents several different nations — some illiterate and untaught, and some, although deprived of a higher education, had been accustomed to a far better life, but through misfortune were obliged to seek this "Home of the Friendless." It has the right name; there is little friendship within its doors, and were it not for outsiders, they would be friendless indeed. There was but one who cried over wiping a cup, for want of strength in her hand, and she, in less than twenty-four hours, was using, for her own purpose, an eight-pound flat-iron, without shedding a tear. It was hypocrisy. I call things by their right name.

There are quite a number of very old people in this institution, who, if kindly treated, are all right. An infant can be soothed by kind treatment, and many of the very aged require the same loving, forbearing treatment. There are very few exceptions. The law of kindness, wisely administered, will make both parties more happy.

I now began to make final preparations for my trip to Washington. It will not be necessary to go upon the third floor. I well knew what awaited me there, and I furthermore knew that I should not go through the cleansing process the third floor required, though I said nothing. My goods and paintings were removed quietly to the house of a friend, and I was ready to depart. My means were limited, but I had a few articles to dispose of. One article of my own workmanship was very nice, and I proposed that several ladies buy it for a present to the pastor of the church of which I was a member. One lady who belonged to the committee of the "Home," and was a member of the same church, forbade the sale of the article, for the reason that I had left the "Home." This was charity on a Pharisaical scale, that, if weighed in the balance, would be found wanting. I at once withdrew the article, sold it to a friend, and started for Washington. I was sure I had plenty of friends there, who knew of my labors and standing during the war. I found them, and was made to feel at home. Now, don't you see that Lawrence won't give up the ship, and that no inferior can put the yoke upon her neck — she was not born for that. There are some people, I believe, born to fight for the right, and as my lot has always been a scene of changes and fighting for the right, I think it will continue to be so until the last life battle is fought — like my distinguished ancestor, who relinquished the ship only with his dying breath.

Now my work began in Washington. I called upon the lady who had my matters in hand, and found that nothing had been done of any account. She at once accompanied me to the Capitol to find the papers that had been deposited there for a number of years.

The records of the first room were searched in vain, the second room also. My friend said, " You will have to make out new papers." "Oh, no," I said ; "they dare not throw such papers into the waste-basket ; my papers are here." My friend said, " You go into such a department, and if you cannot find them, call for me. I'll rest here a few moments until you return." I went, and to my great satisfaction, I found the papers. Instead of taking my own matters in hand, the year before, I left them in the hands of those whose neglect looked like want of interest in the matter. Also my going to the " Home " was for selfish purposes.

I did not expect to enter it, if at all, under a year or two. ·There were eleven to be removed by death, before my name would be called, and but one of that number passed away before I was called to take her room ; that movement threw me out of several hundred dollars. And why were efforts made to get the papers out of my hands when I was at the " Home ;" and threats made that my room " would be taken away if I were gone more than four weeks?" These things speak for themselves. I asked a lady of standing and influence why it was that they did not have a lady of intelligence and at least some refinement at this institution? She answered, " We cannot procure su:h a person." What is a home for? Is it not to feel at rest, to be treated kindly? The law of kindness will fight more battles for the right than overbearing rudeness and cruelty. Some persons do not prosper with the power given them, just because they do not know how to use it, but are sure to abuse it. I have taken my share of suffering abuses without resentment until forbearance ceased to be a virtue. I do not believe in Northern slavery. It is time that it comes to an end; and if every Christian man and woman would come out against the wrongs of the present day, and take a decided stand against them, we might be looking for the Millennium ! But, such is life; where one takes sides for the right, too many oppose and persecute it.

I was in Washington through the long session,

which did not adjourn until late in the summer, doing all that was necessary to be done.

General Curtis had written a favorable letter to Gen. Tracey, a member of Congress from Albany district, who worked the bill through, and I obtained my pension. Just previous to this, Congress had passed a bill allowing all nurses $12 a month and no more. I was one of the first nurses and passed through all the hardships of the war, but failed to present my case among the first, owing, as I have said before, to my being hurried into the " Home " a year or two sooner than I expected to be. But by stratagem and perseverance I effected my escape from the so-called " Home," for which I thank my heavenly Father.

It was a long time before I could consent to bring my life before the public, though I had often been importuned by friends to do so. I always claimed to adhere to the third verse of the sixth chapter of Matthew : " Let not thy left hand know what thy right hand doeth." But the time has come for me to work with both hands, for it is a God-given right. When in Washington attending the " Grand Encampment " of the Grand Army of the Republic, which took place in September, 1892, I was again urged by friends to write the history of my life. A lady editor from New York came to me while there, to have me prepare a sketch of my work during the war. This I was not able to do under the excitement of this occasion. The nurses were invited to some entertainment every evening, and through the day were off at sight-seeing. The gentleman, Mr. Wright, with whom about thirty of our lady nurses were stopping, hired a very fine conveyance, with six beautiful gray horses, to take us to Arlington to visit the graves of our brave boys, some of whom I knew and cared for. On our return we were invited to lunch at the New York Avenue Presbyterian Church. We had a most delightful time all through the encampment. Our superintendent, Miss Dame, president of the Nurses' Corps, at Washington, made us feel at home through her untiring efforts and kindness. She had two tents prepared for us on the white lot, where we met many of our boys that we once cared for; and here we had a most delightful time. After our lunch at the Presbyterian church we were entertained by a pathetic song, and remarks by Mrs. Fowles on the death of some of our soldier boys.

Our stay was one continued scene of pleasure, and will long be remembered by us all.

CHAPTER XV.

"It kindles all my soul,
My country's loveliness."
— *Cassimir of Poland.*

Soon after the close of the war I was invited by my friend, Mrs. Draper, to visit her at her home in Worcester, Mass., and accompany her to Boston,

where her husband, who was a member of the
Legislature, was then stopping. Worcester, we all
know, is a beautiful city, and my hostess was an
ideal entertainer; therefore, my every moment
spent here was full of enjoyment. My little Fanny
was with me, and being an exceedingly pretty child,
with a very romantic history, attracted no little
attention.

On a lovely spring morning we took the train for
Boston. The air seemed full of the teeming fra-
grance of the resurrection of nature. Everything
looked peaceful and holy. What a contrast to the
four previous springs. Even the birds were happy,
and from each little throat came forth victorious
notes which seemed to say, "Make way for
Liberty! Make way for Liberty!!" Everybody
and everything rejoiced, and involuntarily I found
myself repeating the beautiful lines of Thompson:

> "The first of heaven's blessings;
> Sweet Peace, how delightful thou art!"

Arriving in Boston, we were met by Mr. Draper,
who took us to the House of Representatives, and
into the Governor's room, where we were introduced to Governor Andrews, the justly-titled War
Governor of Massachusetts. The Governor then
presented us to each member of his staff. Here we
met the Hon. Edward Everett, a true and noble
gentleman everywhere. He told us he was to give
a lecture that evening on the causes and issues of
the long and bloody struggle through which we had
just passed, and which had left so many mourning

homes in every State of the Union, and cordially invited us to hear him.

During his discourse little Fanny grew weary, and fell asleep in my arms. The speaker noticed it, and, pointing to the child, said, " Behold one of the innocent little victims of the war ; a beautiful, helpless orphan, now quietly sleeping in the arms of her foster mother," drawing a comparison between this child, who had fallen to the care of a motherly heart, and the many hundreds of just such children made orphans in the same sad way, who had found no friend to supply their needs, or gentle hand to guide them in the way of right.

After finishing our visit in Boston, we went to Auburndale to spend a short time with some very dear old friends, Prof. George W. Briggs and family. Prof. Briggs was at that time principal of Laselle Seminary. Mrs. Briggs, before marriage, was a Miss Lydia Laselle, one of a large family, who from my infancy had been our neighbors and friends ; consequently, I looked forward to my visit at Auburndale with much anticipation. I was not disappointed. During my stay here the professor said to me one day, " You certainly must not think of going away without going to see Nathaniel." This was the Rev. Nathaniel Laselle, then pastor of the Presbyterian church at Ames. Here we had another good visit, and Rev. Laselle, who was well acquainted with the poet, Whittier, thought I ought not to leave Ames without meeting him. Accordingly, he accompanied

me to the poet's house, where we were very hospita-
bly received by Mr. Whittier and his maiden sister.
After a pleasant and entertaining call, both gentlemen accompanied us to the station and we returned
to Auburndale.

Shortly after my return there was to be a gathering of the old anti-slavery element at Faneuil Hall,
Boston. We were all intending to be there, but
unfortunately Mrs. Briggs was ill at that time and
unable to go, but as she would not hear to any
sacrifice being made on her account, Mr. Briggs,
Fanny and myself attended the meeting, which was
addressed by Wendell Phillips, Wm. Lloyd Garri-
son, John G. Whittier and others.

I had been invited to address a relief association
at New Bedford, and Mr. Whittier kindly gave me
letters of introduction to the mayor, and to the
Howells and Tillinghasts, the last two families being noted and influential " Friends."

From New Bedford we went to Hartford, Conn.,
to visit the editor of the Hartford *Courant* who
had been one of my patients in the hospital at
Fairfax and at Bishop St. John's place. His wife
came to the hospital to help care for her sick husband. We became very good friends in " Old Virginia," and they urgently insisted that I should
visit them at their home in Connecticut.

While here I attended the Congregational church.
After service, the pastor, Rev. Mr. Burton, invited
me and my little girl to dine with him and his
14

family that afternoon. After dinner he asked us to go with him to the Methodist Sabbath-school where he wanted Fanny to sing. She sang Sabbath-school songs and sang well.

On our return home something in the man's voice and look attracted my attention. A new idea dawned in my mind, and stopping on the walk I turned upon him suddenly and asked, " Mr. Burton, what is your Christian name, please?" "Nathaniel," said he, " Nathaniel Burton." " And what was your father's name?" " Henry Burton. He is a Methodist minister." " And preached in Middleburgh years ago?" said I. " He did." "And do you remember a girl by the name of Catharine Lawrence?" " Well, is it possible? I guess I do remember Catharine Lawrence, and I recognize her now. My father and mother must know of this."

This recognition occurring on the street, with both of us standing as if spell-bound, must have looked odd enough to passers-by, but I thought nothing of that then, only that I had met an old acquaintance. On reaching home, Mr. Burton immediately wrote and dispatched a letter to his father, who was living in Middletown, Conn., and on the following day the father came over and nothing would do but Fanny and I must go home with him, where we had another good old-fashioned visit.

On returning to Hartford, Mrs. Isabella Beecher Hooker sent her carriage with an invitation for us to spend the day with her, but as we were already engaged for the day we could not accept it. The following day she came herself, and carried us off to her beautiful home. In the afternoon she took us in her carriage again and drove to her sister's, Mrs. Harriet Beecher Stow's, where we made a long and pleasant call. In the evening we were driven back to Hartford, well pleased with our day's entertainment.

Our next visit was in Bridgeport, where at an entertainment at the church parsonage we met by chance two relatives of little Fanny's, her father's cousins. They called upon us next day and learned all that I could tell them of the sad fate of Fanny's parents and how I became possessed of the three little daughters.

On leaving Bridgeport we turned our faces homeward toward the old Schoharie hills, feeling that the change and recreation had been in many ways a blessing to us both.

CHAPTER XVI.

"The rough burr often contains a sweet kernel."

REMINISCENCE OF A FRIEND.

A few years after the war I went to Washington, intending to spend some time, and took up my abode at the Woman's Christian Home.

The first morning after my arrival, on entering the breakfast room, I was introduced to a large

number of ladies, among the number several
Southerners. After the compliments of the morning, I found myself seated between two of the
Southern ladies. One leaned a little forward and
asked the other if she wanted to see another
Yankee. " No," she replied, with an oath, " I never
want to see another Yankee." I was between two
fire-eaters. I must retain my powder until I could
take good aim. I met them each morning after
that with some pleasant salutation, as " Good
morning, ladies; I hope I see you well," ignoring
their past sharp-shooting. After a time I missed
Mrs. Fisher — the lady who never wanted to see
another Yankee — from the table, had not seen her
for a day or two; finally I asked where she was,
and was informed that she was sick. Her room
being directly opposite mine, I thought I would
call and see how ill she really was. I rapped at her
door. She bade me " Come in." " Good morning,
Mrs. Fisher; I heard you were sick. Can I do anything for you?" " Oh, yes, Miss Lawrence. Bring
up a chair and sit down by me," and handing me
her Bible, said, " Will you read a chapter for me?"
" Certainly; I am only too happy to do so." " I
am so glad you came in. I am sick and lonely."
After reading the chapter, I asked, " Had her
friend, Mrs. H., been in to see her?" " Oh, no; I
don't think she cares for sick people. Only Mrs.
Bent and the doctor have been to see me. Mrs.
Bent brings my meals. And now that you have
come, won't you stay all the time you can?" No

use for powder here. Lawrence holds the fort. "Now, Miss Lawrence, I have something to communicate to you; I think you may be able to help me. It is this: my father, in his will, gave me the old homestead. I married a doctor and left the place in the care of a man whom I trusted for honesty. As long as my husband was living all went right. When the war broke out my husband was appointed a surgeon-general in the Confederate army, and near the close of the war he died. I was left without means, and resorted to my parental home for help. The man refused to recognize any claim of mine whatever. He said the property belonged to him, and he could do nothing for me. My next step was to take counsel of a lawyer. I had no money to pay a lawyer, but hoped he would take the case and take his pay out of the estate. I went to Warrington, Va., and laid my case before a lawyer. He referred me to another, the second to a third, and so on. I had made the round, not finding one willing to espouse my cause. I asked the last one to whom I applied how many lawyers there were in Warrington. 'Forty,' he replied. 'The lawyers in this city, *forty* in number,' I said, 'must be the relics of the 'Forty Thieves' in the Arabian Knights.'" "Well, Mrs. Fisher, had you presented the case plainly, with a prospect of gaining the suit, they doubtless would have taken the matter in hand."

Then she asked me, " Do you know any Northern lawyer who you think would take the case for me?"

"I know of but one who would be likely to do it, and that is Gen. Butler. He is a real Yankee and will not put on false colors. The Southern people know him quite well." "Yes, we do know him *quite* well; but I have just a mind to go and see what he can do for me. He will know I am a Southerner of course, as my property is in Virginia. I am a little fearful. Tell me how I may approach him." "You go to his office. As soon as you enter you will be directed to a seat. There may be quite a number of applicants before you. When your turn comes, a gentleman will ask you what he can do for you? Tell him you wish to see Gen. Butler on special business. If the General is in, you will be directed to his private office. Then tell him all, correctly, and you will soon learn what your prospects are. Now, Mrs. F. be careful how you approach him. Call him by his title name. You must be a lady, and don't let that Southern fire blaze up. Keep cool, even if he should say something which does not come up to your expectations. If there is hope in your case, you may be sure you will gain the suit. I know of several apparently hopeless cases which have been won by Gen. Butler."

Mrs. Fisher was an invalid and subject to crutches, but very energetic, and in a short time she was on a street car, *en route* for Gen. Butler's office. On her return I perceived the mark of disappointment on her countenance. She said, "I did not see Gen. Butler, he was not in." "Who

did you see, and what is the result of your visit?"
" When all others had passed out of the office, a
gentleman came to me, and asked if he could do
anything for me. I asked if Gen. Butler was in his
private office. He answered, 'Not at present, but
you can state your case to me; that will be all right.
It all passes over to him.' He of course learned
that I belonged to the South, and asked, 'Could I
not find a lawyer nearer home, who would understand the case thoroughly?' I said I was informed
that Gen. Butler never lost a case. He was such an
old fighter he would stick to his client like a blood-
hound until he gained his suit, and in this case he
would have blood-hounds to fight with. He
laughed all the time he was talking to me. I really
felt vexed at the man." " When are you to see
Gen. Butler, or to know the result of your visit?"
" I left my number, and after the case is investigated he will write me. He asked who recommended me to Gen. Butler? I said, a Miss Lawrence, from New York. She knew of several suits
he had gained for working women in Lowell,
Mass." "And you missed seeing Gen. Butler?
Mrs. Fisher, what kind of a looking gentleman were
you transacting business with?" " Why, he was
quite advanced in years, and bald-headed, somewhat portly, and would laugh at almost every word
I said. Once I said, old Ben Butler, and he laughed
until he shook. I do not think he is a special
friend of Gen. Butler's. I'm sorry I missed seeing
the General." " No, you need not be sorry. The

gentleman you saw was none other than Gen. Butler himself." "Oh, no, the gentleman said he was not in his private office." "Of course not, he was in the public office when you went in, and you, being the last one, you were just as private as if in the other office." "Now, Miss Lawrence, if I get back my old home, I want you to come and live with me." "Well, Mrs. Fisher, do you think the Southern fire-eater and the Northern Yankee could live harmoniously together, and enjoy life?" "Oh, yes, Miss L. couldn't you?" "Yes, most certainly I could." The hatchet was buried.

There appeared to be now perfect harmony at the Home, and I proposed that after Miss Wicks had asked the blessing at the breakfast table, each lady should repeat a verse from the Bible. The proposition was pleasantly received and carried out. Miss Catharine Bent had been directress of this home since the war. She was a lady of intelligence, and well fitted to take charge of an institution of this kind. This was not a Christian home in name only, but a place where the Christian virtues were cultivated and practiced. It has been a *home* for many a homeless one of both North and South.

My business in Washington having been accomplished, I left for my own home in New York, with the heartiest of good-byes and the kindliest feeling of my companions, even the Yankee-hating Southerners.

I never met my friend, Mrs. Fisher, again, but

afterward learned that she never regained her paternal home. Her declining life, which was short, was pleasantly cared for at the St. Elizabeth Institution at Anacosta, Washington, D. C., where she quietly passed away.

CHAPTER XVII.

" Rule kindly, tenderly,
Over Thy kingdom fair."—*Mulock.*

One of the most discouraging and dangerous practices in a school or family is partiality among the children. With the teacher it is not so much to be wondered at, as a beautiful and pleasant child will make its way with the world, but it does seem almost impossible that such a feeling as preference can exist in a fond mother's heart ; or, if any, it would seem that the most tender feeling would go forth to the child least favored by nature, that the tender pity for an unfortunate one would draw it nearer to the mother heart than are the ones who need no pity. But such is not always the case.

Among the friends of my early youth was a lovely girl who married well, and whose home I frequently visited. Although everything was done to make it pleasant for me, I often felt greatly pained to see the devotion of the mother to one beautiful child and her apparent coldness toward one more plain. On my first visit there were three children in the family, Nina, a most beautiful, bright-eyed little fairy of five years; Lucy, a very plain little girl of three, and a baby boy.

I soon perceived that Nina was her mother's idol. Her imperial beauty had quite beguiled the mother's heart. Whatever she said or did was just the thing. Her mother never wearied of fondling or caressing her, and she was constantly addressed as " My darling," " My beautiful," " My beloved," etc., while Lucy was never anything but plain Lucy, unless she was called a tiresome child, or something of that sort. If she chanced to lean up against her mother, it was " Lucy, do go away ; you tire me to death," or " Do go along, Lucy; you are forever in my way."

Although she was but a mere baby, I could see that poor little Lucy longed for her mother's love. Her great, hungry. pleading eyes touched my heart. How one loving kiss or affectionate caress would have cheered the drooping child. One day when her mother had pushed her away with the oft-re-peated phrase, " Lucy, pray do get out of my way," I ventured to say, " Mother, little Lucy is hunger-ing and thirsting after a mother's love." The mother replied, " Of course, I love her well enough, but she is always in my way, and such a tiresome child."

Two years later I visited my friends again. The same spirit permeated the household. Edward, or Eddie as he was called, had grown to be a fine child, the son of the family, while beautiful Nina —

and she was peerlessly beautiful — was an imperious
miss of seven, who received the homage of a queen,
and as a queen made a subject of her sister Lucy
in every sense of the word. Lucy was a patient,
silent child, keeping mostly by herself, her great,
mournful eyes looking like wells full of unshed
tears. My visit was not pleasant. My heart ached
for this little stranger in her parents' home. Still
two years later an epidemic of scarlet fever swept over
that neighborhood, and among the stricken ones
were the two little daughters of my friend. Both
were very ill, but when the crisis came, Nina turned
for the better, but Lucy did not improve. No one
spoke to the child about her condition, but she
seemed to understand it all, and towards the last
called her mother to her bedside and said, " Mamma,
everything in heaven is beautiful, isn't it ? " " Yes,"
her mother answered, " very beautiful." " I knew
it," said Lucy, " and if Nina had died she would
surely have gone there, but I am so glad she is
going to get well, for, dear mamma, I feared it
would kill you if Nina died, and I prayed God to
spare her to you, and, mamma, does the Lord ever
find any place for homely little girls like me, do
you think? I know I have always been so much in
your way, do you think I would be so much in the
way of the angels that they would not let me stay
there ? " " My dear child," said her mother, " the
Lord looks only at the heart ; if that is good and
beautiful that is all He asks." " Is that truly so,
mamma? " " It is truly so, my darling," said her

mother, who for the first time in her life saw that her child, in heart, was truly beautiful, and with a great throb of love, stooped and kissed her. "Then," said the dying child, "I am so glad to go, and, dear mamma, when you and the rest come, maybe some-where among the angels you may find me."

"IS THERE ROOM IN ANGEL LAND?"

Is there room among the angels
  For the spirit of your child ?
Will they take your little Mamie
  In their loving arms so mild?
Will they ever love me fondly
  As my story-books have said?
Will they find a home for Mamie,
  When she's numbered with the dead?

Chorus.
Tell, O, tell me truly, mother,
  E're I join the shining band,
Do you think they'll bid me welcome,
  Is there room in Angel land ?

I have sorely tried you, mother,
  Been to you a constant care,
And you will not miss me, mother
  When I dwell among the fair.
For you had no room for Mamie,
  She was ever in your way;
And she fears the good will shun her,
  Will they, darling mother — say?
                Chorus.

I was not so wayward, mother,
  Not so very, very bad,
But that tender love would cherish
  And make Mamie's heart so glad,

Oh, I yearned for pure affection
In this world of bitter woe,
And I long for bliss immortal,
In that land where I must go.

.   Chorus.
Tell, O, tell me truly, mother,
E're I'm taken from your hand,
Do you think they'll bid me welcome,
Is there room in Angel land?

CHAPTER XVIII.

' Woman, dear woman, sublime as thou art,
In the shadow of thy Lord must thou sit."

WOMAN SUFFRAGE.

How much women have already done for their
sex. I well remember when the wife was often left
destitute of support after her husband's death although the bulk of the property came through her
by heïrship before marriage, and after by hard work
and raising a family. The husband had a lawful
right to will the property all to his children or
others as he might choose, leaving the wife destitute
of any means, except the hold of affection she
might have on the children or other friends.

I distinctly remember the case of one very respectable and good woman, who bore to her husband sixteen children — some of them died in their
infancy, and some years after the death of her
husband. In her feeble old age, the daughters-in-law

tired of caring for her and she was finally taken to the county poor-house and died there.

Women have worked until they have a law upon the statute books of the State of New York that married women can hold their own property and their children, if the husband is a worthless man, not able to support them. Quite a privilege.

How the lives of such women as Susan B. Anthony, Elizabeth Cady Stanton, Amelia Bloomer, and many others have been dedicated to the work of bettering humanity, and especially the lives of their sister women, and how unflinchingly and untiringly Miss Anthony, Mrs. Mary Seymour Howell, and many more did work during the early part of the year '94, endeavoring to give to the women of this State the right of suffrage, not because it would make women more masculine, but because they well knew that if women could speak through the ballot, some of the evils of our land might be wiped out. Some of the traps which ensnare our sons and daughters into sin and ruin might be sprung or broken. And how have they succeeded? The Constitutional Convention convened at our capital city, Albany. This convention is expected to do much toward reforming the laws of the State, and to frame such measures that vital questions may be submitted to the people on election day.

Among other measures to be looked after is the Woman Suffrage question. I attended the sessions. Long strings of petitions signed by both men and women were presented to the convention to show that not only women, but some of our best and most eminent men thought the measure just. Many eloquent speakers, both men and women, labored in favor of the measure, showing much good which might arise from the use of the franchise in female hands. After one exceedingly convincing discourse by a God-inspired woman, one prominent member of the convention remarked, as we were passing from the assembly hall, "How gladly would I give a thousand dollars if I could have the power and ability to deliver such a discourse as that." "Another meeting at the Assembly chamber," said a friend to me. "And what is that?" I asked. "Oh, it is an anti-suffrage meeting. You don't want to go." "Why not?" "You may not like their sentiments." "Well, I shall go for all that. It's best to hear both sides of the question; then you can judge which you like best, but I am firmly set in the right of woman suffrage. There will be some of our talented ladies of Albany take part. I am sure I shall hear something nice. I shall certainly go, as I do not wish to miss one of these meetings as I am always benefited."

The appointed time came. The Assembly chamber was well filled. The first speaker was introduced. His discourse was lengthy, but not at all severe. The next was an Albany gentleman. He gave a good talk on the subject, but it was rather aged. It must have just awakened out of a thirty years' sleep. Call it "Rip Van Winkle." Now, thought I, the next will be a lady. But in this I was disappointed. Up sprang a little object, which looked like — something I dare not mention. He spoke fiercely. He said women had too many rights already. His speech was a burlesque on womanhood; yet a committee of women calling themselves anti-suffragists applauded him.

Who are these anti-suffragists, and what have they done? Let us look after them a moment. They style themselves, "Albany's Exalted Four Hundred." Whence their origin? They certainly are not the sons and daughters of the aristocracy of former days, but the latest mushroom growth of these last *fast* days. They are the descendants of the "veneerings." Has not the revealed truth come to us, in glaring colors, that a score of their number are to-day paying the penalty of their money-grabbing instincts within our prison walls? And where did they procure that long list of names on their petition? Go search the slums and pur- lieus of our city and you will find many of the names which appear on this petition. These poor degraded wretches, whom good women would gladly save, have, through their own ignorance, sealed their own doom.

Who were the special committee appointed to consider the suffrage bill? and how did they con- sider it? They exhausted much eloquence and time, and finally concluded it would not be safe to let the women come in. Like Demetrius of old they cry out, "If we let the women vote many of our crafts will be in danger." The shrines of the Goddess of the Ephesians must not be meddled with by meddlesome women. Where is the man—I would like to ask—who would willingly license women with the power to pull down those institutions which he loves and patronizes? Not the members of this committee sure. No, they say, we must not let this question go before even the *men* on election day. We must squelch it.

CHAPTER XIX.

"Soldiers, rest in heavenly bowers
While we strew thy graves with flowers."

MEMORIAL DAY, 1895.

Here am I in the beautiful young city of Oneonta, on the eve of the 30th commemoration of the close of the war of the rebellion. How different from the years of war when the recruiting officer was the most prominent object to be seen on the street, when the booming of every cannon in the South rang a death knell in some human heart. When carnage and tears and groans filled all our country.

Now all is peace and prosperity, and all the present generation knows of those troubled times is what they read from books, and papers, or the mythical tales told by some of the "old soldiers."

Sabbath morning I attended service in the new Universalist church, where the G. A. R. and all

15

kindred societies came by special arrangement to listen to one of the most beautifully and poetically patriotic sermons that it has ever been my good fortune to hear. The Rev. Edward Foster Temple is one of God's truly gifted ministers, and to listen to such a sermon as he preached last Sunday morning means to bear away with you an impersonation of the speaker and the sentiment of his discourse to wear forever in your memory.

In the afternoon the Y. M. C. A. and the Christian Endeavor societies congregated at the First Baptist Church where Christianity and patriotism mingled throughout an interesting service. In the evening a union service was held in the First Presbyterian Church, where the Rev. Mr. Hall delivered an eloquent sermon.

All the week has, in a measure, been dedicated to preparations for Memorial Day, and at last, on this eve of this one day of the year, can be seen dozens of lads and lassies wending their way homeward from the fragrant woods, laden with baskets and bundles of vernal beauties teeming with the untrammeled purity of the sylvan bowers from which they were culled.

This is right. Lay the pure flowers of nature on the breast of the man who went forth in the purity of his young manhood, to brave a war and lay down his life to preserve for us a free country and a united nation.

And now the Memorial morning breaks in splendor. The happy birds sing of freedom. The very atmosphere is permeated with the spirit of peace and harmony. Presently the bands begin to play, and I get a comfortable seat, where I can see all to advantage. The procession heaves in sight. The gaily caparisoned marshal proudly leads. The bands play beautifully and sweetly. The Third Separate Company makes a fine display. The fire laddies, in bright uniforms, almost dazzle the eyes. Daughters of Veterans, Relief Corps and other orders make up a fine cavalcade, and behind all this comes a little handful of G. A. R., who fetch up the rear, marching to the cemetery to decorate the graves of their comrades who have answered to the final roll-call, who have finished their warfare on earth and laid down their arms in peace.

As I muse on the pageant before me I am carried back to the old days, and wonder if this little remnant is all that is left of the hundreds of stalwart men who went forth to battle from this stirring town. Are we to decorate the graves of all but these? Oh, no! There were many whose graves cannot be decorated, for they sleep in the malarial swamps of the South, or lie buried in forgotten places on the sunny hillsides, and many white bones have bleached on Southern soil without the rite of burial. These are not strewn with flowers to-day, but they are no less hallowed in the hearts who loved them.

But why is this small reminder of that terrible struggle placed at the very latter end of the procession? Is it that their faded blue shall be seen

in greater contrast with the gay uniforms which
have preceded them, or is it — can it be true — that
the "old soldier," to whom we owe all that is free
and beautiful in our country and government, is
being slowly, but surely, relegated to the rear; that
the aspiring generations of to-day, who are enjoying their rich inheritance, are forgetting the brave
old soldiers who gave it to them?

It seems so little time since I helped to care for
our sick and wounded boys that I marvel to see
them look so old and feeble, so gray and worn,
until I start to rise to my feet, and find that I, too,
am like the rest, old soldiers, old nurses, all passing
on to that realm whence only the bugle-call of the
archangel "can awake them to glory again."

CHAPTER XX.

"Sweet Auburn! loveliest village of the plain,
Where health and plenty cheered the laboring swain."
— *Goldsmith.*

In September, 1894, I found myself in the town
of Oneonta, almost a stranger in a strange land. I
had but one acquaintance that I was then aware of
in the town; but as ever the good Lord had me in
His keeping and opened up the pleasant places. I
came — as some people would say — not under the
most favorable circumstances, for I came as a book
agent, a being whom some persons appear to dread
or be afraid of. I had a book, a "Life Sketch" of
myself, which I wished to dispose of.

Of course I first called on my friend, where I was made very welcome and where my attention was drawn to a beautiful pair of twin boys less than two years old, the only children, and the decided pets of the household. I have laughed till my sides ached to see these babies run, jump, dance, play leap-frog and—fight. Probably many a mother will think, Oh, these twins don't compare with mine, for I am told that this young city in the Susquehanna valley is famous for twins, boasting of a dozen pairs or more, but as I gazed on this special pair, John and George, I thought here lies a portion of future America. Who knows what responsible positions are in store for these exceptionally bright babies, and what pit-falls lie in their pathways. I almost shrank in thought at the weight of responsibility resting upon my young friends, the parents of these boys. What an infinite amount of patience and wisdom will be necessary to bring up these boys to fill their places in life, with honesty, sobriety and the love and fear of God. In the babies of to-day lies the future of our nation. Heaven grant that the children of this generation be so brought up and instructed that the future of our nation shall be one of progression in all that is good. I soon discovered that I had several old acquaintances in town and secured a boarding place with one on Academy street. Here all was done that could make my stay pleasant and homelike, but the town being large and extending over large territory, in order to shorten my daily

walks I have changed my place several times and
have lived with people whom I had never known
before, but have received only kindness, and right
here let me say that if I am ever asked what
Oneonta is noted for, I shall answer, "For its
hospitality to strangers." For since I came here so
many hands have been stretched to me in friendship and sympathy that it seems as though everybody stood ready to give me a lift in the right direction, and I shall bear away with me the fondest
recollections of the place and its people. Especially
do I feel deepest gratitude to a lady friend with
whom I boarded, for extreme kindness and attention in sickness and for sympathy and consideration
at all times. She is a woman who is an active sym-
pathizer with all reforms and a hard worker in the
cause of temperance ; but was never too busy or
too weary to be solicitous for my comfort. May
God bless her and prosper the cause for which she
works.

CHAPTER XXI.

After my return home, I thought a good while
about the matter of writing my life work, and
finally set about it, and have done what I could, as
my health and strength would permit. I have
given the sunny side of my life to the public with
as much care as possible, hoping that those who
read, may read with charity, whatever may not
agree with their views of right, as I have given

C. S. LAWRENCE.
1893.

nothing but real life. Every life is made up of sunshine and cloud, and we can enjoy as much of
either as we will. I think I have more sunshine
because I will not permit the cloud to predominate.
I seek the light which every one may have if they
will receive it. There is no need to go through the
world with long faces to frighten children and make
every thing look dark around them.

As I was at one time teaching a class of young
ladies, I was taken with pleurisy. My lady assist-
tant became very much alarmed; she stood before
my bed with mouth wide open and a pair of large
black eyes extended, saying, "Oh, Miss L., don't
die!" The sight was so ludicrous that I gave a
shout of laughter that drove my pain away as
quickly as it came. My cousin was standing by my
bed asking what doctor I wished. I said, "Jane
Shaw! my pain has left me." She says, "Kitt, you
have cheated me." "No, indeed; I did not, I was
in perfect agony at every breath, but the comical
look of Miss Shaw caused me to shout and the pain
ceased." Even in pain we can make it pleasant by
a little sunshine. Some may be ready to say that
some of my remarks are personal; well, if they hit
the right ones, that is all right — we should take
things that belong to us, as we have a perfect right
to them. If there was less deception in the world
there would be less sin to answer for. I regret to-
day for having done so little good in the world. I
can look back over my three score years and ten
and see so many niches that I might have filled.

Oh, so much more good I might have done in working for the Master!

I have presented nothing but the truth. My childhood is written mostly from memory — some things being handed down to me by those who were actors on the scene in my babyhood, and as I have always had a love and a great charge of children, I thought this part would please and amuse them. I have never lost my interest in them, and I love them next to my Saviour. A friend asked me if I were permitted to choose employment in heaven, what would it be? My answer was: A group of children to look after among flowers. They were the Saviour's pets, and those who do not love them here will, no doubt, be greatly annoyed if they should get to heaven, for they will find hosts of children there. There are many wrongs to be corrected according to our views, and many life battles to be fought, and many hills to climb. Oh, if we have the moral courage to right the wrongs, and fight the battles, and climb the hills, we might be a blessing to the world while in this life and heir to an inheritance in the life eternal.

In giving this sketch of my life, I hope my friends will excuse me for not going into all the details of it. The greater part of my life has been devoted to teaching children, as has been already stated. The seed scattered in early life is more sure to take effect and grow into usefulness in coming years. Children should be trusted with tender loving care by teachers as well as parents.

That poem that speaks so beautifully to all ages, I must quote:

> Speak gently to the little child,
> Its love be sure to gain;
> Teach it in accents soft and mild,
> It may not long remain.

And next to childhood comes youth, that period of greatest anxiety to parents, an age of restless ambition to themselves.

> Speak gently to the young, for they
> Will have enough to bear;
> Pass through this life as best they may,
> 'Tis full of anxious care.
>
> Speak gently to the erring, know
> Such may have toiled in vain.
> Perhaps unkindness made them so;
> Oh, win them back again.
>
> Speak gently; it is a little thing
> Dropped in the heart's deep well,
> The good, the joy that it may bring,
> Eternity may tell.
>
> Speak gently, it is better far,
> To rule by love than fear.
> Speak gently; let not harsh words mar
> The good we would do here.

Next to mothers are teachers, who help to fill the niches, and bear, at least, a small part of the burdens of some over-burdened mothers, and thus fulfill the Scriptural command — "Bear ye one another's burdens."

I have no sympathy with those mothers who devote their time to teaching poodles and carrying them in their arms as their favorite pets, and leave their babies to the care of unskillful nurses and servants.

This is, indeed, an era of changes, and many sad ones come to all. I find, in working for the Master, that there are many ways of approaching the erring. The most effectual is by love and kindness; these will often win the most obdurate. I wish to relate an incident that occurred in my earlier years: I was once called upon to go on a mission that put my inherited heroism to a severe test. A family became very much reduced in circumstances, through sickness and misfortune. The father was a clergyman. He, with his wife and four children, were to be provided for. Now, I thought, I will call on Judge ————. He is a wealthy and influential gentleman, but always averse to beggars, as he called them, and would sometimes treat them harshly. I called — the lady was sick and the judge was out. I had a pleasant visit with the lady, who gave me three dollars. She said, "You may keep this from the knowledge of the judge, and get what you can from him." In a short time he came in. "Good morning, Miss L., this is the first call you have ever made us." "Yes, sir. Judge, I have come to the Court of Appeals." "What is it?" he asked. "I have come to beg." "Well, you understand your business. Do you know how I treat that class?" "Yes, sir; but if you put me out the front door, I'll come in through the back door." "Well, well, you are a chip of the old block. What can I do for you?" "Well, I want any thing that a needy family can use — provision, money, wood, food for his house, etc." By night there were large quantities of everything needful gathered into the minister's house, woodshed and barn. Twenty-five dollars would fail to cover the cost. This was, indeed, a good day's work. But I prayed earnestly before I made my morning visit.

I now close this little volume, praying that the Lord may bless this, my last work, and that my friends may meet me where the weary rest from labor, and that we may all together enjoy "that rest that remaineth for the people of God."

> Speak gently to the aged ones;
>   Grieve not their care-worn heart,
> The sands of life have nearly run;
>   Let such in peace depart.